DOWN THE OCEAN SUMMER '64

A Novel

Michael Wright

With Gratitude:

For Ben Herman, Barbara Wernecke Durkin, Edward Cohen, Ira Mazer, Ellie Finlay, Eli Wright and Hannah Wright.

Hat tip: Barbara Hetrick and William W. Linthicum

Editorial sensei and Cover Design: Elena Carrillo

Formatting by guru Frank Christel

ISBN 978-1-5323-8994-8

PREFACE

THE "MERLIN" DIALECT

Down the Ocean (pronounced Downey Owe Shin) – Summertime destination, meaning: "traveling to Ocean City, Maryland."

Also used to indicate any destination: down the store, down the shore, down the way.

Online source: A brief tutorial — The "Merlin" Dialect — www.robinsweb.com/maryland/merlin.html

> *The Merlin Dialect is spoken by a mixed population which inhabits a triangular area on the western littoral of the Chesapeake Bay, bounded roughly by a line commencing at Towson's Toyota, then westward to the Frederick Mall, thence following the western border of the cable TV franchise and the string of McDonald's along Route 50 to the Bay.*
>
> *Because of the numerous words and phrases common to both Merlin Dialect and modern English, linguists have long postulated that there is some kinship between the two.*
>
> *Speakers of Merlin Dialect are all able to understand standard English from babyhood, chiefly because of their voracious appetite for television. However, they invariably refuse to speak standard English, even with outsiders who obviously cannot understand a word they say.*

VOCABULARY

Ballmer — Our city

Merlin — Our State

Arn — What you do to wrinkled clothes

Bulled Egg — An egg cooked in water

Chest Peak — A large body of water nearby

Colleyflare — A white vegetable

1

IODINE AND BABY OIL

It was all Della's fault.

If she hadn't broken up with him like she did, with that "I think we need to see other people" line, things could've been completely different.

"We need," she'd said, meaning she did. He was happy with things just as they were but no amount of reasoning and argument could convince her that she ought to be as content.

This is what Roy was stewing about as he drove on Maryland Route 50 toward Ocean City, going "down the Ocean," as it was phrased by Marylanders. It was still dark; he'd left Baltimore at three a.m. to be on the beach just after sun up to have a full day of it. He had to be back to work the same night for the 11-7 shift at Sparrows Point, Bethlehem Steel's vast plant. Every minute was a race.

Jesus, he thought: July 4th weekend and I have to work. Run down the Ocean, race back to the Point.

Dwight, Della's brother, was in the passenger seat yammering on about his latest theories about why the Orioles weren't likely to beat the hated Yankees over the weekend.

"I mean, let's face it, between Pappas pitching and Boog on a home run streak, you'd think they could be out in front by thirty games, but nope. Not with Bauer managing. He's one of those guys just can't finish. You watch. They're going to need a ammalance by September," Dwight said, his Baltimore accent mangling "ambulance."

He proceeded to run through all kinds of statistics to prove his points—statistics Roy knew were at least half made up. Dwight resided on his own little planet and that was fine, but for the moment Roy wished Dwight would go to sleep. Even more, he wished Dwight was Della. But Dwight had sworn up and down he'd figure out how to find Della, so Roy brought him along.

She was down the Ocean for the weekend with her girlfriends, a bunch of crazy females who screamed at and fake-fainted over guys on the street—or flipped them off. Why couldn't she at least hang out with normal, quiet girls? Roy just knew they were having wild parties, orgiastic riots of unbridled hedonism. It drove him nuts to think of Della with any other male, let alone at the center of a whorl of drooling guys.

So there he was, driving hell-bent for three hours before sunrise. He was going to track her down, prove his steadfast adoration and win her back.

They'd been together for over a year, having met at the local teen center in Dundalk, the suburban sprawl outside of Baltimore, where Roy lived. Actually, it was her cousin Melissa he was attracted to at the start, but she lived in D.C. and only came to Baltimore every other weekend.

Melissa was petite, blonde all the way down to a tiny bit of unshaven fuzz visible on her thigh just below the hem of her mini-skirt. She was one of those bold girls that Roy and his buddies always leapt toward, hopeful of legendary sex—or any sex, for that matter.

Most of the girls at the teen center roosted on the bleachers, giggling and whispering, or dancing only with each other, seemingly indifferent to masculine allure. They were entirely too much work for not much return.

Not so with Melissa—she lofted a smile Roy's way and in less than thirty seconds they were on the dance floor, shaking it down.

Della was more reserved, old-fashioned in many ways, like her name. She was the plain best-friend-type who often tagged along with an untethered Melissa-type to be her anchor and safeguard. Roy thought she was just okay; nice enough but no Melissa with those caramel candy tanned legs.

Once Roy and his buddies melded with the two girls Della let her goofy side out and his opinion of her lightened. He was amazed when he discovered they were going to the same high school. It was a huge school but they traveled in different worlds—he in the academic track, aimed at college, she in the commercial track, being readied for a job in business someplace. Still, he couldn't believe he hadn't noticed her.

Roy resurfaced from his reverie, the highway licking under the tires, bugs pinging off the windshield. Dwight was offering him a piece of candy.

"No thanks."

"Sugar's good for energy," Dwight said in his official I-know-everything voice.

"Maybe. I get sleepy from it."

"That's weird."

"Yeah, well, guess I'm weird, too, Dwight" Roy shot back. He softened his tone: "I mean it's cool—Deuce," using Dwight's preferred nickname. Roy was Riff when the two were hanging out, but only with Dwight. It was just a buddy thing to make Dwight happy; Roy had no intention of being known as Riff anywhere else.

Dwight shrugged. "Shit, man," he said, gobbling the chocolate, "more for me."

Roy sighed, relaxed his grip on the steering wheel for a moment and kept the pedal down as far as he dared.

A DJ's voice came through a surf of static on the radio. "Okay, cats and chickies, here they are: The Supremes, rocketing up the chart with 'Where Did Our Love Go?'"

Yeah, Roy thought: where?

When Melissa couldn't come to visit for a second weekend in a row, Roy almost ditched teen center. His senior year drinking buddies, Phil Camber and Johnny Monkton, pulled him out of his funk, sharing a fifth of vodka as they drove through the quiet Dundalk neighborhoods. The streets were wet with the last thawed remnants of a late January snow.

He discovered Della sitting alone at the top of the bleachers, looking like an unclaimed child at the state fair.

"Hey," he said, with a cockeyed smile.

"You," she said with a grin, "are a shameless drunken bozo."

"Damn righ'."

"Well, you better sit down before you fall down."

He glanced at the bleacher rows behind him and realized he was swaying. He sat in a heap, quickly.

"How much did you guys drink?"

"Nahmuch," he said. "Fifth."

"God, Roy, you're like that comedy guy who pretends to be drunk."

"Don't know him."

"He was on that show with Dean Martin a few years back."

"Don't know it."

He gave her a sidelong glance.

"Wait—are you trying to fool me?"

Roy popped up from his slumped posture with a bright smile. "Yep."

"You goof. You had me worried. I thought you were going to get caught and thrown out, banned forever and me with you."

"Nah. I was just kidding around. I got you, huh?"

"Yep. Got me good." She reared a fist back and brought it slowly to his chin. He did a slow motion knocked-out collapse.

The speakers began blaring "The Twist."

"Come on," she said, "get those dancing feet going."

They quickly reached the floor and started twisting amid the dozens of other couples.

"We look like worms trying to get out of an apple or something," she shouted in his ear, cracking them both up.

The evening flowed on. They danced, got refreshments, talked. Phil and Johnny hollered at him to come with them but he waved them off.

“Come on, lover boy Romeo,” Phil shouted.

“Nah, I’m okay here. You guys can get a ride with Rondo, I saw him outside grabbing a smoke.”

“Okay, there, Castronovo,” Johnny yelled.

“That’s Casanova, you idiot,” Phil said and baffed Johnny on the back of the head.

They made their exit, shoulder punching and squabbling. Roy shook his head. “Those guys’ll lower your IQ just by being in the same room,” Della said, laughing.

“Phil’s cool. Johnny, well, he’s just Johnny. I’m glad you were here tonight, Della.”

“Yeah, me too. Almost didn’t come.”

“No? Me, too!”

The Lettermen Song, “When I Fall in Love,” came on. She came into his arms without a word. Roy’s throat went dry the instant their bodies met.

Later, he took her to Ameche’s. It was a drive-in burger place with order consoles, car hops and a constant parade of guys showing off their wheels, racing the engines at top volume as they cruised the lot. Roy was showing off a little—it was the more expensive of the local hang-outs. With Melissa, the choice was Gino’s where the burgers were 15¢ and the circling cars were a bit less noisy.

As they chatted over burgers and onion rings, Roy began to recognize how greatly Della’s light had been overwhelmed by her cousin’s breathless nova. He also realized her eyes were swimming pool blue.

When the restaurant lights started shutting off, they realized nearly two hours had passed in a flit. Roy was amazed at how easily they’d talked throughout the time and how different she was from Melissa—and most other girls.

Talking with Melissa was usually in one of two categories: teasing banter or arguing over why she didn’t think they should go “all the way.” Melissa was all about torment—sexual promise leavened by very quick, very strong hands. It was all the more frustrating because some of the bleacher girls had made a point to whisper to Roy's friends about Melissa. How when she still lived in Baltimore she ran wild with all manner of boys—even married men. He couldn't understand. Why not with him?

But now, this Della? She was clearly a nice girl. Somebody he'd take home to meet the parents, that kind of nice girl.

He pulled up in front of her house. They sat in the quiet, radio off, engine ticking as it cooled. Roy was feeling conflicted about going behind Melissa's back and he was pretty sure Della was too. But when he leaned toward her she didn't hesitate.

Their first kiss set loose feelings he didn't know how to name; he drove around for hours afterwards.

Kissing Della was sweet, soft. Melissa was jittering intensity, all tongue, panting attack then sudden retreat.

When they told Melissa she took the news gracefully; she even seemed glad, which further galled Roy. Screw her, he thought. Better yet, un-screw her—I hope she never gets laid again.

They became Roy&Della at Dundalk High, dating all through spring of '63, his senior year; she was a junior. They were together in the hallways between classes, on weekends, at sports events, each other's proms—inseparable.

When he found a job selling shoes in the evening, it was to her house that he'd go with his after-work snack, feeling completely at home in the family living room. In time she started working at a women's clothing store in the same mall and they would leave the work day together, like an old married couple.

Although they were both looking forward to the freedom of warm days and evenings, things started to unravel a bit once school was over. Roy was putting in a lot of work hours, trying to save up for college while Della was cutting back at her job, wanting to enjoy her last summer before her senior year and emergence into the real world.

Finding time to be together became difficult. Out of the blue Della started spending time with a set of new friends, wild Baltimore City girls, who kept late hours and ran around like lunatics. That was how he saw it, especially after Della told him about things they'd done, like drag-racing on the streets and taking on a drinking challenge to show up a carload of snooty girls from Towson, the rich kids' suburb.

One of her friends had actually mooned a cop.

"Are you kidding me? Jesus-god, Della!"

"What? The cop just laughed. Don't be an old fart."

Roy tried to act cool about it for a time, until he couldn't any longer.

"I don't think these girls are good for you," he said without preamble one evening.

"Why not?"

"I don't know; they just don't seem like regular girls."

"What's a 'regular girl'?"

"You know what I mean."

"I don't think I do, Roy. They're great girls and if I want to hang out with them I will. They're my friends."

So that was that and he didn't dare push it.

In late summer, things finally simmered down a bit. It took longer than he liked but at last Della had gotten a bit weary of the steady go-go-go of her friends; she eased into making more time for him. They fell back into summer moons, wandering walks and making plans for their life together.

When September eclipsed the lazy days, he started at Essex Community College and things began to wobble again, except now it was Roy who became the rare sighting.

He hadn't realized how greatly he'd be caught up in college life. He tried to explain.

"Look, they're showing movies—foreign films! I never knew they existed!—they do plays, poetry readings! They bring in these speakers. I mean crazy, great stuff: people talking about 'ban the bomb,' 'equal pay for women'—you'd like that one, right?"

"Yeah, it sounds great for you but I can't be out on school nights; you know how my parents are."

At the same time, Della's life had become centered on after school clubs: yearbook, homecoming, senior prom committee. He understood; her senior year should be as great as it could be. But he felt uneasy, as if they were breathing different atmospheres.

The fatal blow came in early November, when she announced what "they" needed.

"Other people!" he exclaimed. "I don't want to see other people, why should you?"

"I just do," she said, arms folded across her chest.

"That's a stupid answer."

"Oh, thanks very much."

"You know what I mean. It's those girls you were running with. They got inside your brain. You're not like them."

"I'm not? How do you know?"

"I just damn do."

"Well, I don't think you know anything about me at all, then," she said, in a haughty tone that told him this was not a winnable debate, though he tried mightily over many long hours in person and on the phone to persuade her.

He was devastated. They had once talked marriage and now this? Some sick demon had flipped a switch on him: bang. He ranged from anger to a hollowed-out state of contempt for everything. His days were pewter colored; he started cutting classes constantly—what was the point? Della didn't love him, didn't need him or want him around, so why the hell should he be anywhere else where he didn't matter? Screw school, screw all the bullshit. He quit his job at the shoe store and took to just driving around in the evenings, his mind a blank.

After being tormented in Algebra II by a professor he detested—and it was mutual—Roy went over the edge. He broke a classroom door by slamming it with all his might. He paid for the repairs, then dropped the guy's class.

He knew he was in a shitty place but there was no helping it—everything was against him.

He was shooting pool with a friend one afternoon in late November, cutting German, another class he hated.

They were in the basement of a bowling alley around the corner from school. The guy upstairs, a practical joker, hollered down: "Hey, you guys better come up here and see this. The president's been shot."

"Yeah, sure, Tony," Roy called back.

"No, I ain't jokin'. I think they just said Kennedy died. Get up here!"

His heart broke when Kennedy's death was confirmed. Watching news anchor Walter Cronkite trying to hold himself together when he announced the horrible reality was like seeing the world ending. Days of helpless gazing at the television followed. After the funeral, with all its depressing pomp and the sight of JFK's kids and Jackie being brave, Roy felt as if he had fallen into a bottomless chasm.

His fall semester's D- average was hardly a surprise. He just wanted to fail everything and be swallowed up by the earth. Why he even bothered to sign up for spring classes was beyond any point he could figure out.

"Trying to please my parents, I guess," he told Phil Camber one night when they were aimlessly cruising the loop between various burger drive-ins. "Pretty funny considering neither of them went to college and they're doing okay. Hell, my father never finished high school and he's a boss at Sparrows Point."

"Yeah, well, working for a living ain't no party, believe me. I'm just saving for Maryland. If I can get in next year, I mean. They have this summer course thing you can take to qualify if your high school grades are like mine."

Roy nodded. Privately he tended to shake his head over Phil's obsession with the University of Maryland. Phil thought going to community college was settling for second best: he had fantasies of walking the grounds of College Park in a letterman sweater: Big Man on Campus. Good luck, Roy thought, well aware of Phil's weaknesses as a student.

Now, though, in this summer of '64, with Phil at U of M actually taking those remedial summer classes, Roy thought maybe the guy might make it after all. Time would tell, as Roy's dad liked to say.

"Usually state trooper speed trap up at that curve," Dwight said, breaking into Roy's recollections.

"Got it," Roy said, slowing down.

He tossed a cigarette he didn't remember lighting out the window, watching the sparks spray in his side mirror. Hell with it, he thought, start a forest fire, who cares?

Well, he did, but he was struggling with the reality that they were driving down the Ocean on this particular mission. Ocean City was paradise for him, for people his age, where they could run free and be wild. He'd been to Atlantic City a number of times with his parents—it was just tired and overrun with family crap—and Rehoboth, just north of Ocean City, was like some retirement home. Just driving across the Delaware state line made him drowsy. His vision of rescuing Della from herself had turned OC into a bewildering chessboard, overrun with uncertainties.

"We need to get some breakfast, Riff," Dwight announced. Roy called Dwight "Deuce," as requested, and had opted for "Riff" when Dwight insisted on tit for tat. Riff was the leader of the Jets in the musical everybody was crazy about.

Roy could live with it and the nicknames helped to remind he that he was only hanging around with Dwight for Della sightings. Great ploy, he told himself acidly: make friends with the brother. You might as well come by to bake cookies with her mom, you dipshit.

“Yeah, okay,” Roy said. “Let’s not be too long about it.”

“No sweat. Anyway, I know my sister well enough—she don’t roll out of bed ’til noon if she ain’t working.”

He didn’t know if he wanted to eat or not. His cigarettes had taken on the vile sugary taste they got when he was exhausted. Anyway his stomach wasn’t fully settled from the previous weekend when he’d gotten stumbling drunk and puking after consuming a six-pack of malt liquor and a big bag of beer nuts.

The beer nuts were to help modulate the consumption. That was the plan. He had just wanted to get drunk enough to get through another overnight shift of sweat, boredom and grease reek at the mill. Instead he was barely able to navigate the first few hours of his shift, reeling from one hiding place to another, decorating each with copious outpourings of masticated nuts. Thank god the bosses were all busy attending to some injury accident in the 42” mill; he was assigned to the 56” mill that night.

Passing the curve and seeing no cherry tops, Roy picked up speed again and lapsed back into his thoughts.

The break-up turned him into somebody that exceeded his usual self-contempt. He began to follow Della around on the sly. He ended up trying to spy through the windows of a house she was visiting one evening. He had no clue as to who lived there but in his mind it had to be some conniving seducer.

The blinds were drawn in all the windows. He crept around the house, trying to peer through any opening he could spot until one pane showed him his own face, clenched with jealousy and fear. He ran straight back to his car and cried until his throat was raw.

Tormented to total distraction, he dropped out of school in the fourth week of the spring semester. His father used his boss prerogative and finagled Roy a relatively cushy job.

It was perfect: quality checking massive rolling-pin-like cylinders used to reduce the gauge of head-high coils of steel.

It was repetitive, mindless, robotic, though shift work screwed with his body clock. When he wasn't working he was asleep or wandering around to places of happier days, hoping for some sense of the familiar, for a glimpse of something that could lift his heart again. But everything eluded him; even the arrival of The Beatles on the "Ed Sullivan Show" had failed to cheer him to any real degree.

After the beer nuts night, he kept the alcohol in moderation, only wanting to be numb enough to stave off thought. It didn't occur to him to go in search of a new girlfriend. There was no point—he would absolutely win Della back in the end. It didn't even matter to him that she wouldn't talk to him any more. He tried to use visiting Dwight as a pretext for getting in the house, hoping when she saw him there it would trigger the old memories but it was no use. The new Della seemed to have no give to her. He was allowed to drop by, knock on the door, wait on the front sidewalk for Dwight; that was the limit.

Okay, he thought, bring on the challenges, girl—I'm up for it.

"This place is sposta be good," Dwight said, waving his hand in front of Roy's blanked-out face. It was an all-night burger joint at the end of town, good as any other. And it didn't matter: they'd arrived, they were down the Ocean.

After eating, they changed into their bathing suits in the urine-reeking john. His breakfast hadn't gone down well; it was a plateful of grease with two desiccated yellow eyes staring up at him. Dwight had several stacks of pancakes, washed down with three glasses of milk. He had a chipped tooth that gave him a jack-o-lantern look and chewed with his mouth wide open while he talked and interminably talked, now about the Colts.

"This year, all the way, you wait and see if I ain't right. Johnny U, man," Dwight was saying. "Raymond Berry. Are you kiddin' me? Like the perfect pair on the field. Berry always catchin' that ball with his toes in bound, falling out of bound. I mean, we're talkin', like, poetry in motion."

Roy just nodded and said "Uh-huh," over and over, though he did feel like telling Dwight that poetry had three syllables: it wasn't "poitry." But, oh well.

Reaching the beach just as the Atlantic was starting to tinge pinkish, they spread out a blanket and watched the sun rise. The day was going to be hot, there was no doubt about it. They stretched and yawned and fell to their own portions of the blanket. The sand was cool and damp through the fabric; Roy scooted himself around a bit, making a body impression. Sleep fell on him like a crashing wave.

The sun was almost directly overhead when Roy woke up with a start, disoriented. The beach had blossomed into a multicolored swarm. Bodies of all descriptions lolled, walked, chased after balls, ran tumultuously into the water—like some movie scene.

Roy sat up, watching, mouth dry, eyes feeling sanded. Dwight was still conked out, mouth agape, snoring. Roy stood shakily and stretched. His body immediately clamped down, skin grabbing sharply against the movement. He looked down at his legs, pink on top and white in the back.

Roy was fair-haired and pale. He stood there, gazing gravely at the roll of the ocean, feeling the sun's sting on his exposed skin.

It took a moment for Roy to realize that Dwight was standing next to him.

"We need lunch, Riff."

"I need to get in the shade, Deuce. I'm pinking up here fast."

"Nah, you can't go hidin'. Not if we're goin' to track Della down. I know what you need: iodine and baby oil."

"Never heard of that."

"Yep. Baby oil keeps the skin protected and all that; iodine gives you good color and it heals you at the same time. Great shit; I use it all the time. Brown as a nut." Dwight stripped his shirt off and made a turn.

Roy had to admit: Dwight was indeed brown as a brown nut.

"Guys at the place tease me I'm half-colored," Dwight joked. Roy winced. He hated racist crap—there was more than enough of that at the mill every day.

They folded the blanket and waded through the hot sand to the boardwalk. Every other blanket they passed had a transistor radio on it and all of them playing "Where Did Our Love Go?"

Roy sighed.

There was a store on the boardwalk that sold pretty much everything under the sun a few blocks down. Roy kept his head on a swivel as they walked along, searching for Della in the passing throngs.

Purchases in hand, they found a spot in the shade, and applied the concoction. Roy hated the pore-clogging feel of the liquid but his skin did seem more pliable. After stashing the blanket in the car, they headed down the boardwalk to Thrashers to stuff themselves on the justifiably named "Famous French Fries" and sodas.

While they ate, Roy kept surveying the steadily trodding mass along the boardwalk, hoping for a glimpse of Della or any of her friends. He didn't know if Melissa had come along or not; he kept seeing petite blondes in the mob and decided to take it as a sign. He had to find Della, that was all there was to it. Do or die, he told himself, I'm going to win her back.

Dwight raced through the biggest bucket of fries they sold and bolted off to buy another one. The guy was a walking pit. Roy shook his head, embarrassed once again at his decision to start hanging around with him.

Dwight was the perfect definition of uncool. Best thing he had ever come up with was "Deuce" as a nick-name; he was Dwight Junior. His clothes were from second-hand stores and in the worst imaginable colors, he had stifling body odor at times—women fled from him two minutes into any exchange. He had a dead-end job pumping gas and fixing tires at a gas station, living in Dwight World where if only he could catch that one break he'd be hired as a sports announcer or even a team's manager.

"Manager," Roy snorted in private. Dwight was twenty-five and still didn't have a driver's license due to some issue with taking the written test.

He didn't hate Dwight or even put the guy down that much. Tolerating him was Roy's notion of redemption. This weekend, though, Della would see Roy's kindness and near-saintly compassion for Dwight, remember what a great guy he was and fling herself, penitent, into his arms once again.

It was worth being a conniving asshole.

Nothing mattered except getting back together; the break-up ate at him like a beast from some Greek myth plucking his guts out day after day.

What drove him craziest was the timing of the break-up. It just didn't make any sense to him.

Everything had been going along great, especially in their time alone. They kissed their lips numb and explored each other, but Della was steadfastly against oral sex and intercourse. For a while he didn't mind but after too many nights of driving home with an ache that could only be relieved in his own bed, he began to press her.

One night they'd been in his car, windows fogging up in the late October chill, a big Halloween moon pulling at them, and something had come over Della. They'd been groping each other senseless for an hour. Roy was murmuring in Della's ear about how badly he wanted her.

With a sudden violence that scared him, she had yanked his hand tightly between her thighs and said "God, yes, Jesus, yes, yes, yes," sounding like such a complete lunatic he'd jerked his hand free and stared at her, speechless.

A moment later she burst into tears and turned away from him.

“I’m sorry, Roy.”

“It’s okay.”

“Really; I’m sorry.”

He kissed her shoulder and patted her back. She leaned into him and they sat there, silent.

Roy knew that was it. She’d come to some last turning point of passion, couldn’t resist him any longer. He knew they’d move into real sex the next time they were alone.

But, somehow, no. The air around them clotted, closed. Della put him off for several dates. When they did get together, she began begging off kissing him due to some gum ailment she wouldn’t explain. She wasn’t even willing to sit with him in the car, choosing to invite him into the house where his chances were zero.

Had she scared herself? Had she been threatened by him pulling his hand away in abrupt panic? Did she think he judged her? That he was ashamed in some way for her, of her? He didn’t know how to approach opening the subject with her.

Worse, he had no experience. He was a clueless virgin. He had no idea how things were supposed to go if she shifted course again and gave in. Would she go totally insane and devour him? His parents had given him no instruction, neither had school. He didn’t tell her this, of course. Guys were supposed to be in charge, after all.

Eight days later she dropped the bomb on him. “We need.” Jesus.

He couldn’t get through to her, so he kept tabs on her as best he could. He talked to her less discreet friends. She wasn’t dating, they told him, mostly running around with that bunch of girls. She didn’t even go to her senior prom, they said; that really broke his heart since she’d been on the planning committee. He called and called but she wouldn’t talk to him, see him.

Immediately after graduation, she went to work for a bank downtown. One day, he passed by the bank, trying to see how she was doing—to see what she was doing. He slipped inside when things were especially busy and watched her for a while, doing something with a tower of folders at her desk. His heart rose up with pride; she looked so competent. Another look around punctured his adoring heart: she was surrounded by a horde of square-jawed young banker guys, all looking right out of Esquire with their perfectly creased everything and pristine hair cuts. He knew they were all surreptitiously checking her out—his Della—plotting, lusting, horny as baboons.

Dwight was waving his fingers in front of Roy's face. "Earth to Roy, I mean, Riff," he said. They were loafing in the shade around the corner from Thrasher's

"What?"

"I think I might have the address for where they're stayin' at," Dwight said, letting out a prodigious potato-y burp.

"Why didn't you say so?"

"I forgot until just now."

"Well, let's go already."

The place was six blocks away. Roy could feel his reddened skin drying up again.

As they got closer, all his fears were turning real. The apartment buildings were becoming less touristy and more downbeat; this is where the real Ocean City people lived, the kids who were in on the beach scene. Bicycles and beat-up barbecue grills littered alleyways behind the houses, trash cans overflowed with bottles and beer cans—memorials to debauched parties. Surfboards were visible everywhere, as were sea-bleached blond surfer boys and their tawny, indolent females. Exactly the kind of world he wanted to protect Della from.

At the address, they stood perplexed. It was a small bungalow somewhat dwarfed between two apartment houses. It looked abandoned. He pushed past Dwight and knocked sharply on the door. No answer came; the place was empty. Or more like emptied, as if some unspeakable crime had gouged out all the humanity it may have ever possessed.

Roy knocked again.

"I was pretty sure this was the right address," Dwight said in a small voice

Roy walked around the house. In back there was a patio and a place to hang laundry, but there was no sign of life there, either. Considering it was Fourth of July weekend, it was completely weird that no one was in the place.

Dwight stood on the sidewalk, toeing a drift of sand. "Well, shit, Riff."

"Yeah, shit for sure."

"Ha, that's good: 'shit for sure.' 'Shit for sure'."

"Christ, Dwight, you're just useless."

"Hey, I was goin' by what I was told. I mean, maybe I got the wrong number or wrong street but where we are is what I remember. Anyway, I'm Deuce, not Dwight, man."

"Yeah, okay, fine, Jesus-god! Is there any place she'd be likely to hang out?

"I don't know. The beach, I guess."

After banging on doors up and down the street, then walking blocks to parallel streets with the same address they gave up. Roy marched toward the beach, Dwight trailing behind, babbling excuses. They walked for hours, scouring the boardwalk again, the amusement centers, the pier with all the rides. Nothing.

Time loped past. They would have to leave soon if he was to be in Baltimore again for his shift. He considered calling in sick, but Roy would have to be in a coma for there to be sufficient reason not to go to work with his father watching on —an irreversible coma.

As they walked in hopeless circles, he remembered a vacation with his family in Atlantic City. He was fifteen and not happy about having to let his little sister, Leanne, tag along.

What he wanted was the freedom of the boardwalk for himself, not to baby-sit.

Along the way, he met a freckle-faced girl who made it clear she was very interested in him. After flirting him halfway to combustion she suggested that he should try his luck at a spin-the-wheel game. To his amazement, he won a big pink fuzzy dog for her and was rewarded with a swift kiss on the lips, quickly followed by excuses about a curfew and the sight of her back and the pink animal vanishing into the evening crowd.

He was about to make a comment about being taken for a sucker when he saw his sister's face. Her mouth was scrunched up, her eyebrows were lowered; she was mad as hell; worse, she was hurt.

"Ah, come on, Leanne, it's okay."

"You didn't even know I was there," she said with all the resentment in her 10-year old body.

"Sure I did. Here, look, I'll get you a dog, too, okay?"

"Yeah, fine, okay. But you didn't even know I was standing there."

They went back to the booth and Roy went through all of his money without winning anything. They walked back to the boarding house in silence. He wanted to drop through the boardwalk and burrow down to bedrock. How could he have ignored Leanne like that? For some stranger, some flirt who was just a—what was that old fashioned term?—a gold digger.

The guilt he felt was a cold knot in his stomach that didn't go away for a week.

What he felt now was the same sickness magnified by a thousand. He was failing at the most simple possible thing he could imagine. He was letting Della down; if he couldn't save her from the kinds of mistakes her cousin and friends were known for making, what was the truth of his love for her? He was useless and no kind of man at all.

Yes, okay, this disorganized search was not a well-thought-out plan, but what difference did that make? Shouldn't they simply find one another because it was fated? This wasn't going steady in high school any more, this was real life and he was failing miserably at it. And to top it off, he was stuck with her doofus brother until returning, when he would shove the chipped-tooth jerk out of the car. All he could picture was desolation after that; a landscape of unending gray and silence.

There wasn't anything or anyone on earth that he didn't hate.

As a last resort, he drove up and down the streets, hoping to spot Della or anyone who might be part of her group of friends—or anyone at all. Dwight was keeping up a running commentary on the qualities of the girls they were passing.

"Nice bongos on that chest!" Then shouting: "Hey baby, can I play a tune?"

The girl flipped him off with both hands.

"Don't know what you're missing, blondie!"

"Dwight, cut it out."

"Check out those turd-cutters on her, man. Jesus, how do they move their asses like that?"

Truly disgusted by now, Roy was tempted to abandon him.

Finally, driving across the bridge away from the city, everything a blur to his

stinging eyes, Roy admitted utter defeat. He silently cursed the fates. It was really over.

He immediately began hatching the next plan to get Della on his side but hopelessness painted black x-marks over each idea. The road ahead was a running movie of Della being ravished by an endless stream of savage surfers and bankers and him alone, bereft, destined for nothing.

An hour outside of Ocean City, Roy realized something was wrong with his ankles. He pulled over at a gas station and saw red, bloated hams where his feet had been. The heat from the engine was flowing across his toes like an open oven. Roy leaned forward and felt his entire body crinkle with pain. Whatever sunburn he had suffered in past was only a practice game compared to this. Every inch of him except where his bathing suit had been was a landscape of nettled fire.

"Jesus Christ, Dwight—" he began.

"Deuce, Riff; come on, it's Deuce."

"No, it's not. No, it's more like dumb-fuck. Look at me! I'm a goddam lobster from your iodine and baby oil! I gotta work tonight and I'm so sunburned I can't even turn in my seat to yell at you!"

"Well, shit."

"Yeah, shit. Shit-shit-shit!"

"I mean, it was good for me, I'm as—"

"If you say you're brown as a nut, I'm going to leave you here!"

"Hey, look, you oughta know your own, whattayacallit, toleration."

"Tolerance!"

"Yeah, that."

Roy clenched his teeth, threw the car in drive and sped off toward the lowering sun. The sooner he could get to Baltimore the better.

They rode in silence. After an hour had passed he glanced at Dwight and saw the same look of hurt that had gripped his sister's face in Atlantic City.

"Okay, okay, Deuce. You're right. It's okay. I should've realized."

A few seconds went by, then Dwight spoke: "I'm sorry we didn't find Della for you. I feel really bad about it, man; I mean really shit-ass bad."

"Yeah, well, that's two of us."

"I feel bad."

"It'll be okay," Roy said, wanting to bite his tongue.

"Really bad, man."

Roy groaned inwardly. Why am I trying to make him feel better?

He let it go. He lit a cigarette with difficulty, bending low over his lighter and feeling the flesh of his stomach protest. Normally he liked driving with the windows wide open, radio blasting, but now he wished his car had air conditioning—anything to stop the burning.

When he dropped Dwight off Roy had to spend more time consoling him.

"You did your best, Deuce. Just wasn't in the cards."

Dwight just stood by the car, head hanging.

It had never occurred to him before that Dwight actually had a sense of dignity that could be bruised. It shocked him a little and saddened him as well, knowing how completely he used Dwight and how disposable their trumped-up friendship was.

The drive home was a flow of misery. He called himself every name in the book, cursed any and all gods, and seriously considered driving into the path of an oncoming car or truck.

He pulled up in front of the house, radio quickly squelched. He wasn't quite ready to go in. The engine ticked, fireflies flitted, crickets filled the evening air with their skirring; his skin pulsed painfully, as if it was trying to detach itself.

His parents were in the living room, TV on as usual. He liked seeing them this way as he walked up: through the screen door, like an impressionist painting of suburban contentment. Something he now felt he'd never know. He liked living there, even if they treated him like a kid, but marrying and living with Della had been the plan, and that was up in smoke.

One look at him set them both in motion. He was immediately taken to their bedroom, the only room in the house with air conditioning, stripped to his underpants and laid on a fresh sheet, all the while being questioned about what the hell was he thinking, being in the sun like that.

His mother brought in a bowl of cool water with vinegar in it and began patting him as gently as she could with the liquid. He was completely fried. His face hurt, every part of his body was seething with heat and pain. His father watched on with an expression of concern while shaking his head from time to time over his mess of a son.

By now, Roy had heard it enough that his father didn't have to bother to say it: "You haven't got a practical bone in your body."

Nope, Dad, Roy thought, I never got those bones somehow.

He hoped his father would suggest calling in sick but he knew there was no way. It was like the time in high school when he came home drunk and got caught. His father let him puke his way into hours of dry heaves before finally allowing Roy's mom to administer some ginger ale to settle him down.

"Let this be a lesson to you," his father had intoned in his special School of Hard Knocks voice.

All too soon Roy was driving to Sparrows Point and punching in. Walking in stiffly, holding his breath and trying to keep his skin away from his clothes, he was Frankenstein's monster on fire. He moved carefully out on the floor. There was only a skeleton population and no machines were running; he didn't see any white-helmeted bosses anywhere. He didn't know why he was there since everything was shut down but, holiday or no, this was his assigned shift, so okay, okay, fine.

He found a corner where he could sit on a pile of rags and nod out. Moments later he vomited from the heat and the stench of the machines and lubricants, the decades of grease build-up.

Walking to the end of the mill, he slipped outside where no one was likely to see him. The air felt cooler and breathable despite the ever-present mist of black soot that made the outdoor lights look stippled.

Easing himself down as slowly as possible, he sat on the ground and leaned back, hard hat mercifully lifted from his blistered scalp.

A few stars were dimly visible. The mills were silent.

As he began to nod off, he realized it was past midnight. A new day. Fourth of July.

Independence Day, he thought. Yeah, sure.

2

TURTLE THEORY

Roy was pissed.

It wasn't the fact of the rain. He didn't mind getting wet and at least the rain was warm. It was more the way it was falling all over Ocean City like some snide retort.

Like: screw you, Roy.

Like: sure, Roy, you couldn't wait to get down here because now you're all determined to be over Della.

Like: right, Roy, weren't you were going to do what everbody else does at the shore—weren't you were going to score?

And, sure, since his sunburn was still healing, the cloud cover was a relief, but rain?

He gazed out dolefully at the beach. A posse of junior high-age kids, gleeful and sand-coated, were running around in their soaking wet clothes giggling like ninnies, pasty-faced and smelling like swamp creatures when they passed. Their parents probably didn't even know they were out there; hell to pay when they got caught.

But forget those stupid kids. Where would the girls be? Of course: in the amusement centers, thousands of them hanging out, hoping for, well, him to come along because he had "score" written all over him.

Except he had overlooked something critical. Piled in around the Skee Ball, the pinball machines and the little rifle range where many of the ducks just wouldn't go down, there were also half a million guys, all on the same hunt. You could practically hear the grunting and chest pounding as they leered at the sacrificial virgins.

What made it worse was that the attention was driving the girls into a state of super-shrill manic craziness that pulled the ceiling down around his brain with a steady pour of shrieking laughter.

Worse, they were in—what could they be called, herds? A pride of lions, colony of ants, he thought, maybe a "screech" of girls? No matter: pairs were bad enough. Trying to meet a girl was nerve-wracking for Roy, just in a normal situation. All the insincerity rising out of all the insecurity—it was never easy. When the targeted girl was paired up with her best friend it was always just flat-out tough going. The best friend, usually on the lower end of the attraction scale, always had this "I hate men" look on her face. She wasn't the prize—she knew it and wasn't about to give up the real trophy without a fight. Just walking up to such a duo took more than a few hard swallows.

But herds? Herds were warfare. Either you had to be the loudest idiot in the place, like Donny Spatello back at Mickey's Billiard Parlor, in Dundalk, who would actually drop his pants to get attention, or you had to figure out how to cut a solitary girl out of the flock through stealth.

Roy was not up to stealth. Not on a shitty-assed rainy stupid day like this. What he hoped for was a meaningful look from someone with flirty eyes, then just two minutes of their attention to trot out his act. But with the rain outside and the mating inferno inside, there was little hope. Everyone was at fever pitch and any girl peeling off from their herd was going to be viewed as a little tramp, meaning fair game for every guy, and that didn't seem to be appealing to most of the females.

Ocean City was mostly a place where worrying about your reputation was off the table. Still, without knowing who the guys were and where they were from, a lot of girls were super cautious. Stories zoomed back to your school or neighborhood before you even got home from a careless weekend.

Roy watched the melee a while longer. He knew how it would go. The girls would be leaving in chattering clumps, well aware of being hungrily watched. The guys would start taking it out on the game machines and their hotel rooms later on as the bottles piled up. Worse, there would be those who needed to express their frustrations on another person. He'd been picked on, punched and kicked by similar goons. No need to risk that—move on.

Roy shook his head and walked out into the rain.

"Screw it," he said to a seagull extracting a french fry from a crack in the boardwalk.

He summonsed his Turtle Theory to mind for comfort. When he was a little kid, he and his gang of pals would go turtle hunting and come up empty every time. The next day they'd go out to play Cowboys and Indians and be tripping over turtles all over the place. He told himself: don't push to make stuff happen. Go where the fates take you. And answered: yeah, fine, so long as they take me to score.

He wandered the streets for a while, trying to look like a guy who was totally cool with rain and almost believing it. Cars were steadily circling, as if aimless driving would be a clue for the rain to stop.

On the boardwalk, he came to an intersection where a pier jutted out, packed with various amusement rides and more games. The rides were sitting idle, looking vanquished, their over-bright colors blunted by wet, sagging covers that had seen better days.

An open trash can was receiving a steady flow of water from the roof above it. Fries, hot dog chunks, caramel corn, cigarette butts and unidentifiable bits were swirling atop the water. The can was filling fast from the waterfall. Roy felt himself filling up alongside it, with too many confusing thoughts to sort out.

He had driven down the Ocean on Saturday after a half-day shift at the steel mill, hoping to be late enough to avoid the insane traffic at the Bay Bridge. It didn't matter what time he got there, he was going to sleep in his car at the far end of the beach, past where the motels and burger joints ended.

He was there for the weekend. He was going to find a willing girl, dammit, and lose his virginity in a sex-drenched binge. Out with the old girlfriend and in with anybody else at all: "blind, crippled or crazy," as the saying went.

The bridge traffic wasn't too bad; slow but at least moving. He didn't mind. The view from the long silver loop flung across the Chesapeake Bay always made him catch his breath. He had to be careful, though. Beautiful as the span was, the traffic was two-way, there were no shoulders and the wind could sometimes push a car around like a toy. The last thing he needed was to drift into the oncoming lane, splatter himself and someone else—especially since he was willing to live again, post-Della. Live again and score.

But now he stood in the rain that seemed only be falling on the long isthmus of Ocean City. He was baffled, flummoxed. He'd only brought one change of clothes but he didn't care about getting wet at the moment. The steady soft shower suited the plod of his thoughts.

He didn't know how to move. Not yet. Not with his temples pulsing like this. The salt reek of the ocean was penetrating him, turning him into something with no language, frustration pumping his heart.

Even after everything, Roy had tried to conjure a turtle, to reason with the fates. He was a rubber ball for their amusement, bouncing between poles: yes, he could still get her back; no, it was hopeless.

But the fates didn't have to lift a finger. It was Della who took care of things. He winced at the recollection.

He was hanging around on the Arundel corner a few days after the ill-fated hunt for Della. He loved this little Christmas-garden-like town called Dundalk that was the closest thing to a city near his suburb.

The Arundel ice cream shop was a focal point for local kids; lounging around outside the place was mandatory for establishing one's cool. It was early evening; people had come and gone in the summer heat. A few guys were on the quiet street looking into the open hoods of their customized rides, talking in a vocabulary Roy didn't know or care about: trannies, cubic inches, glass packs.

A carload of tough guys he recognized from the St. Helena neighborhood had drifted past at a tumbril pace, six sets of eyes checking out the corner from within. Everyone froze in place until the car was gone.

One of these days, he thought, I'm going to be spending time someplace where people don't think kicking somebody's ass is just a jolly old fun thing to do.

Roy was ready to cash it in for the night. He knew the St. Helena boys might be back in a while, probably drunk, and that usually meant the door prize for anyone who wanted to have their face stomped and ribs stove in.

He started down the street toward his car and almost immediately saw Della coming out of Kresge's Five and Dime store.

"Well, hey, how about this, huh?" he chirped.

"Listen," she said, her voice an ice pick, "I don't want you stringing Dwight along any more like he's your big pal or something."

"Whoa. Not 'hello' or anything?"

"I mean it. Everybody but Dwight knows what you've been up to."

Roy was staggered by the chill of her voice. "I haven't been 'up to' anything."

"Cut it out," she said, rapidly growing louder, "Melissa called me down the Ocean when you decided to come hunting me like some crazy man, so I drove back here with Angie to avoid your nonsense. When you dropped Dwight off he was almost crying from how you treated him."

"How I—"

"Just leave me and my brother—and my whole family—alone. We are completely done, you lousy jerk!"

She brushed past him, turned at the Arundel corner and was gone. People turned to follow her anger-fueled walk; their heads rotated slowly back to look at him with curious, judging glances. Roy blushed furiously.

What could he do? Chase her down and make her see the, the— The what? The undying love? The true romance of his being? The weirdo he'd turned into, following her around?

She was right: he had used Dwight without the slightest regard for the guy as an actual human. The bit of cooling breeze had vanished—Dundalk seemed to close in around him. His entire body broke into a sweat in the humid air; his face felt hotter than the sunburn.

"Done." "Jerk." Everything was echoing.

Cursing her for embarrassing him in public, he got into his car, drove to the Beltway and just kept the pedal down until he was all the way past Catonsville, the virtual end of the world from his neighborhood. This was his familiar escape, driving to nowhere, radio on full blast.

He turned around and pushed the car even faster. He wanted to be pulled over, to hit the cop and be thrown in jail. For a few hundred yards he even turned his lights off, planning on a fiery crash, then got spooked by the dark and put them back on. He slowed way down and tried to breathe.

The night air was sweet, redolent with the smells of fresh cut lawns and uncountable flowers. Snapping off the radio, he drove in silence; his face was flushed and wet in the dark of the car.

Somewhat eased by the long drive, he got back to his parents' house after two a.m, creeping quietly upstairs to his room. Undressing, he remembered the many nights when he sat with his shirt pressed to his face, inhaling Della's perfume —Jean Naté, she'd told him when he wanted to buy her some— until he was drugged on the citrus sweetness of it. Now all he could smell was his own funk and the woodsy drift of the open field behind the house.

His favorite local jazz show was over, the station, like most, off the air. Even when they were broadcasting he couldn't listen to rock and roll at night—too many commercial intrusions but those didn't matter as much as how rock brought his blood to the surface. Plus, it was the same songs over and over, day and night. The jazz show was always mysterious both for the eclectic nature of what they played and the enigma of what jazz was. There was a conversation going on inside of improvised music that he didn't understand. He could feel it, though, as if there was a untraveled back road in his brain circuitry that improvisations lit up with light from a second moon.

In the dark he fiddled with the radio dial until the station from Chicago came in, slightly staticky like the voice of some dying civilization. It was a jazz station that also played musicians he loved: Coltrane, Miles, Bill Evans, Monk, mixed in with great big band stuff—all of it a soothing blue drone for the middle of the night. He had no idea how he could tune in such a distant station, but there it was most nights, borne through the air magically.

"And here's Cannonball Adderley with Bill Evans and the MJQ from the 1961 album, 'Know What I Mean?,' with 'Goodbye,'" the DJ murmured in a whiskey hum.

The tune came on with Adderley playing an achingly melancholy solo. Its deep longing seeped into Roy's body; tears seeped back out.

Goodbye. Yep. He wanted to move past Della once and for all.

He had to. It was hopeless.

He wanted release.

He wanted to sleep for a hundred years.

Roy blinked—a raindrop had just splatted directly in his eye.

He blinked again. It shook him to realize he was standing on the boardwalk, in the rain, lost in the recollection of the collision with Della and its aftermath.

He felt cut in half. One part had remained, ghosting, in his bedroom, stuck and hurting, and the other was in the here and now of Ocean City, in a state of paralysis, getting drenched, getting nowhere.

He needed to talk to someone. He wished he could call Phil Camber or Johnny Monkton, his best buddies. But Phil was at U of M for the summer, turning himself inside out in the remedial classes, trying to get accepted. Monkton was just gone to wherever the Navy had decided to stick him. Roy couldn't believe Johnny had joined up but there it was, cold fact.

But what the hell would he say, if he could call? "Hey guys, Della hates me!"

Jesus, what a twerp, he thought. No, what was it she called me? Oh, right: jerk. Hey guys, I'm a jerk!

He was so angry with himself, standing there, fists balled, body rigid. What could he do to stop reliving all of it again and again? To stop re-experiencing it as he was now, as one long howl, one sickening smear across time.

He arched back and turned his face upward into the falling rain, wanting to shriek at the heavens.

His mouth opened. Rain came in. He'd heard once that turkeys drowned this way, beaks wide open in a downpour.

He swallowed and swallowed, tasted the sea on his tongue, tasted a memory of kissing Della.

"FU-U-U-U-U-U-C-K!!!!" he shouted with all his might.

He looked around, hoping no one had heard. He hadn't meant to yell. He certainly hadn't meant to curse in public. That was okay around a bunch of guys but not in the world.

He had to move, do something, anything, or his head would explode.

Heading for the street to find his car, he spotted a pool hall and went right for it like something being pulled on a string. This was a world he understood. And it seemed like turtle theory at work in its finest form: the place was called "Terrapin Billiards," with University of Maryland flags hung in the windows. The U of M mascot was the Terrapin, a very happy looking turtle with a big M on its chest. Camber would love this, he thought.

He went in and stood just inside the door, letting his eyes adjust to the light and checking everything out.

The Terrapin was pretty nicely put together, especially compared to Mickey's Billiard Parlor—fancy name for a dingy pool hall, a former store front just around the corner from Ameche's Drive-In. Mickey's was the kind of place only guys would tolerate: unclean, broken floor tiles, a toilet to use only if you absolutely, positively had to . There were dents in the walls where over-zealous players had managed to launch a ball off the table or maybe punished a cue stick for a bad shot.

It was Roy's refuge, a place where he could just be a guy among guys. He played often and developed some skill. Nothing on the level of the local pool sharks but he could hold his own against a lot of players.

His favorite person in Mickey's was "Hoss," a cadaverous remnant of a man who was paid to rack the balls for each table. Hoss always sat half on and off a stool, the wooden rack around his arm, perpetual Camel cigarette dangling from his lips, ashes snowing on his gray sweater. He moved at a sloth's pace but every rack was as tight as could be.

Hoss was Mickey's father-in-law, glad to have something to do, well aware that there was a nursing home hell somewhere with his name on it when he finally weakened. That's how he put it: "Roy, it's a great life if you don't weaken."

Hoss rarely interacted with people except to rack up the balls for the next game. Roy loved the old man for his slow ways and hooded, watchful eyes. Not much got past Hoss;

every amount owed was collected to the penny, everybody playing on a timer got just that amount of minutes and no more. Once, some wise-ass kid came in giving everybody crap. Hoss beaned him with a cue ball and the kid never came back.

Hoss, Roy thought, with a soft smile—a real survivor, that guy.

Roy stepped further into the Terrapin, glancing around, getting the feel of the place.

It was stuffed into what had probably been a burger joint and before that maybe a boutique of some kind and so on back to when it was new and high hopes polished the front window. Still, it was clean and well-lit—and out of the rain.

Standing there, he felt two immediate sensations: the energy coming off a dozen pairs of eyes checking him out, gauging, and then his own awareness that he was in no mood to be messed with after the amusement center and the goddamned rain. Judge at your own peril, he thought, feeling more dangerous than he knew himself to be.

He found a place to sit and watch the players. Most of them were the fumble-finger sort who rested the cue on a half-knuckled bridging hand and tried to play standing almost straight up. Rookies, for sure.

One kid interested him. He had bleached hair that was combed forward kind of like a Beatle, but the hair just stuck out everywhere, as if a white rodent had exploded.

Even so, the kid understood how to bend down to line up a shot, how to make a firm bridge with three fingers on the felt, the index and thumb making a circle for the cue to slide through. He maybe needed some help getting shape on the cue ball after sinking a shot: too often the white ball wandered into a place that made the following shot awkward or even impossible. The kid was decent enough to make some difficult shots but with better shapes he'd have more control of the table.

Worse, though, the kid was flashy, too into his own shtick to be more than just barely above average: dancing around after a good shot, singing with the jukebox (What the hell, Roy silently asked the ceiling: a pool hall with a juke box?), chalking his cue with one hand by rotating the stick between his feet, shooting with a cigarette in his mouth. All very cute.

Roy studied the guy from across the room, glad to be somewhere letting his clothes dry out a bit. After watching for a while, he decided he'd take the kid on if he got the chance.

He moved to where the kid was holding down a table, beating anyone who stepped up, winning consistently. After sitting quietly for a while, Roy started making comments.

"Nice stroke."

The kid ignored him.

"Whoa, lot of draw on that."

More ignoring, though the kid upped his chatter and pool shark flash a few notches.

"Wow! Great combination, man."

Finally, the kid took the bait. "Thanks. You want to shoot some?"

"Me?" asked Roy, king of innocence. "Nah. I mean, I don't know, maybe."

"I'm cool if you are. Loser pays for the rack; bet's two on the six ball and five bucks on the nine."

"Sure, okay, I don't mind, I guess," and Roy put his quarters on the table edge, then watched the kid, who he heard being called Kevin, whup the last few bumbling comers.

"Okay, man, you ready or what?" Kevin stuck a toothpick in one corner of his mouth and his cigarette in the other. He grinned through a corona of blue smoke.

Roy got up slowly, plunged the quarters into the coin thing, then racked the balls. This was different from Mickey's where old Hoss always gave a tight rack. Roy told himself to keep an eye on how Kevin racked in case the guy left the set-up loose. There was a guy in the corner of the place who gave change for the tables and the soda machine but it was clear he rarely left his chair; Roy guessed his weight to be well over 300 pounds.

The tables were bar tables, not regulation, which was good; it helped make long shots a bit closer but a bad thing for 9-ball because the rails were really lively and caroms often knocked the balls every whichaway. This was really true for Kevin, who liked to shoot fast but also hard.

Kevin did well in the first few games; they played pretty evenly, Roy kept himself paced.

9-ball wasn't exactly rocket science—you just needed to sink each ball in ascending numbers, one through nine. Luck was often a factor when the cue ball went all over the table knocking other balls around. Kevin kept up a continuous commentary.

"Yeah, man, this new guy, he's got some stuff, no foolin'. Not likely to choke in the clutch, this guy, no-o-o way." Roy had experienced other players trying to psych him out. Sometimes it had worked, he'd gotten rattled. But not today.

Today, old Kevin, he wanted to say, today I'm pissed off and don't give a damn, loose as a goose, so talk your head off.

After an hour, the kid started losing, raising the bet, making poor shot choices, getting shook up over bad breaks, choking on gimmes. Roy stayed calm, quietly in his own game, watching the kid self-destruct.

Finally, broke, the kid held out his cue.

"Okay, killer, I'm busted. How 'bout we bet this against everything I lost, whattaya say?"

"Nah, come on, Kevin. That's cool," Roy said.

"No, you come on, hot shot. Let me get my money back."

"Yeah, but—"

"Yeah, nothin', asshole. Play or shut up."

Asshole? Hmm, well then. Roy shrugged. "Okay, okay, fine."

The kid racked. Roy sank the five ball on the break, ran the others until he blew it on the six when it bounced back out of the side pocket.

Shot that way too hard, he told himself. Relax.

The kid ran the table and was in almost perfect position on the nine—a straight shot down the rail. He clearly realized people were watching; some impish part of his brain must have been saying: “Give ‘em a little show there, Kev.”

Kevin bent down, wiggled his butt around and shot softly, following the ball along, going “Ooo, ooo” as it trundled toward the corner pocket. At the last second it wandered out a millimeter from the rail, slipped past the pocket, bounced off the point and lazily rolled back out near the center of the table. It was lined up perfectly for the side pocket. Roy could have shot it blindfolded.

He looked at the kid, thinking maybe he ought to suggest best two out of three or something, but the kid was already unscrewing the cue stick, face almost as pale as his bleached hair but still acting out the cool guy part.

“Table’s turned against me, man—warped itself from this rain. And who the hell played ‘Hello Dolly’ on the juke? That old spook’s voice is like gargling gravel.”

A few guys laughed. Most just turned away, the pack abandoning the wounded.

Kevin said softly, just for Roy: “You’re one lucky asshole.”

Asshole; again. “Fine, you little fucker,” Roy said, full voice, surprised at his own vehemence. “Fine. You want to play like some big man, then yeah, I’ll take your stick all right. Took all your money, too, didn’t I?”

Roy stepped into the kid’s space; the kid stepped back, palms up.

Roy turned back to the table, sank the nine, made the kid drop the cue stick on the table by refusing to take it from him. The kid went out of the place, still trying to play it all frosty.

Somebody punched in some buttons on the jukebox and Louis Armstrong came on again, rasping through “Hello Dolly,” with some kid adding, “And goodbye, Kevin.” It brought a laugh to the room and things settled.

Roy picked up the cue halves. He didn’t want to look around, knowing he’d gone a bit far. Screw it, he wasn’t coming back.

But he felt more mixed about this than anything before in his life. He was glad he won, but not glad to win the kid’s cue. He thought the kid was a first-class creep, glad to have shot him down and taught him a lesson. But did he have to humiliate the little punk?

God damn it, he thought, why did it have to rain? I wouldn’t have been in this stupid place if the sun was out. I’d be chasing females all over the beach and after dark I’d be screwing my way out of Della’s life if it took a dozen girls to get there.

He caught his reflection in the window. His face was tight, jaws clenched.

It was growing dark as he emerged from the pool hall. He half expected the kid to be waiting outside to beg for his stick, or maybe lurking with some friends to beat Roy up, but the street was deserted. The rain was still coming down, now in a light dancing mist.

Roy walked to the boardwalk, heedless of the falling water. He’d have to make it an early night—get a meal someplace, change into dry clothes, drive out past the end of the hotels and motels where the dunes were empty of buildings, a place he loved where the sky and ocean made a vast perfect painting in any weather. He wanted to sleep so deep he’d wake up in a new world.

But once on the boardwalk, he didn’t know how to make the next move. It was as if there was nowhere to go, nothing to do but stand again next to the trash can sloshing over with rain water, uneaten food swirling in it.

The memory of a voice crawled into his mind. Mr. Welling, his teacher for World Lit, first semester at Essex Community College. Sitting in front of the class on the first day, all tweed jacket and perfect tie, Welling smiled thinly at them, pausing as he looked each student in the eye, then said: "We'll be exploring the Existentialists. As we do, keep in mind this simple but essential premise: you're all going to die."

Roy's body had clenched in his desk chair as if a door had been slammed in his brain. Until that moment he had never once seriously considered the reality.

He was going to die. No, no, no, but—

But yes.

There was no argument for it. One day, he would no longer exist; he would die.

Welling would die—and soon, Roy hoped. The people in the class were going to, Della was going to die and there was nothing he could do about any of it. He couldn't protect her, his family, anybody.

It, death, was just out there, grinning, hollow-eyed and uncompromising. He felt as if someone had disintegrated all the bones in his body.

It took him many days after that class to come to terms with the idea of it, coming out upside down and so very sad. Why try for love, why pursue a relationship, why bother with any of it—pursue Della, marry, have kids, hold down some job —why?

He struggled with it day after day, so disturbed by everything he saw in the news and on the streets. The break-up, followed by Kennedy's assassination had massively deepened the crisis, nearly provoking Roy to drive to the Bay Bridge and jump off.

Being dumped by Della and everything after was a plunge into a very unforgiving night. The only thing that kept him going was a vague hope that the next day might be better. It wasn't a belief he could justify, given the evidence all around him, just something to hang onto until he couldn't.

Christmas had come and gone, 1964 had staggered in. Roy tried to get going with school in the spring semester but it was no use.

He talked to his parents about dropping out. He blamed it on too many years of continuous school rather than talking about his love life and the weight of death's inevitability. "I just want to take maybe a semester or so off."

They took it in typical fashion. His mom had intuited his mental state from the time of the break-up and gentled him along at every turn. "Whatever you need, Roy," she said. That was mom all the way, ever in his corner.

"Well, you're going to have to get a job," his dad interjected before she could continue. "No way you're just going to lay around here day after day."

When he went to school to drop his classes, he chose to talk to his teachers before going to the main office to fill out the forms.

He was surprised that each of them agreed with his choice. He kept hoping that just one of them would say "Oh, don't go," but they seemed perfectly content to see him leave. So this is what they thought of him? Well, fine, then screw this place altogether.

By the time he got to the last teacher he felt like a condemned man taking his final walk. It didn't help that it was Welling, who just shrugged and said, "Hey, you win some, you lose some and some get rained out," before going back to adjusting his tie and checking his hair in the mirror on his desk.

After a moment of primping, Welling said: "Anything else, Newson? I have class in two minutes."

Roy wanted to string him up by that tie. He had the urge to say, "I have no use for your little baseball cliché, you prick," but kept his peace. He also wanted to tell Welling how greatly the comments about death had greased the wheels to his plummet, but what was the point? Anyway, Welling might have thought it was great—he seemed to think that depressing stuff was cool, somehow.

Now, standing in the falling, chilling wet, Roy actually felt dead, as if the blood in his veins had been replaced by the hateful, cold rain.

It's just sick, he thought. Della craps all over me, I crap on this pool hall kid. Some joke.

"Ha ha ha," he said aloud, mocking every last molecule in the world. He hissed through clenched teeth: "Fuck. Fuck it all."

The trash can was continuing to spill over. He dropped the pool cue pieces into it, where they bobbed a little before joining the food whirlpool in its steady swirl.

He thought a while longer, debating what he wanted to do. Finally, he headed for his car but not to sleep in it. Staying here in the rain and gloom wasn't going to help him any. He had to split, drive home. Maybe eat somewhere on the road if he could find someplace that didn't turn his stomach. It didn't really matter. There was no pleasure in anything anyway. If he was going to feel dead, he might as well sleep like the dead in his own bed. At least going down into that darkness, into the safest oblivion, was consoling in its own way.

Roy trudged down the boardwalk. He passed a hotel that had a second story balcony. Some girls sitting up there hooted at him.

"Hey boy! Yoo-hoo, hey you, boy down there!"

Roy ignored them.

He didn't give a shit. The hell with girls, he thought. And turtles.

3

WAVES

This is it, Roy says to himself. Surfing.

Surfing will give him something more to do down the Ocean than just cruising around and moping about stupid crap.

And surfers get girls.

It all made sense. He's been in love with the Beach Boys since the first time he heard "Surfin' U.S.A." The uptempo songs got him jazzed up—"stoked," as the lingo went—but "Surfer Girl," made him cry in private, filled with feelings of nostalgia he could not explain. There was something about the sorrowful whine of the singer's falsetto that drove him into a state.

Maybe it was in the depiction of the girl, the "little surfer girl"—he can almost see her—so sweet and vulnerable, standing against the "ocean's roar" that affected him. Or maybe it was the promise of going on into some future together. He ached for that kind of love, for that kind of bond. It didn't matter—whenever he heard the song he fell apart.

And, sunburns aside, he loves the beach; even more, he loves body surfing. The thrill of catching a wave and being propelled pell-mell toward the shore, the water roaring in his ears, body in a tumble sometimes—the relinquishment of control—all of it glorious.

So, yeah: surfing.

Besides, he had to be away from Dundalk and memories.

Della had mostly receded in the rearview mirror, though the collapse of that relationship left shadows everywhere. All his hopes for a foreseeable future were diminished, blurred. He began to feel not just emptied out but un-fillable. Whatever he hoped and planned with Della by his side had become a bitter joke and a rapid slide into free flowing anxiety.

He kept trying to land a girlfriend or just a girl to talk with but he was trying too hard, coming on too wounded and needy, yet couldn't seem to stop. He radiated hopelessness, infected the air. All he had to do was turn his eyes in some girl's direction and she would be headed for the door.

Friends from high school he longed to hang with weren't around any longer. People who were just vague acquaintances from his class depressed him when they happened to cross paths. They all seemed to be married, about to get married, having a kid—or, kids; Jesus!—or worked up about some job or stuck in "remember when" about high school. He wanted to yell in their faces, all of them: none of this fixes anything! He held back. After all, in the land of the clueless, he was king.

The only people he talked to on a regular basis were his parents—who consistently confused him with their conflicting notions of who he was or should become—and the guys he worked with at the steel mill. Most of his co-workers were okay; he could talk sports or cars with them but there were several he avoided.

One of them, Calvin, was the stepfather of a girl Roy had gone to high school with. He was a peculiar man, tiny with a pinkish face that seemed hairless and looked airbrushed, with eyes that were always moist, as if he was a perpetual mourner. His eyes seemed to linger on Roy when they crossed paths. He was greatly relieved when he found out that Calvin had left the Point for a different job. The guy gave him the heebie-jeebies.

The other was a buffoon named Simmons who loved to tell the guys in the locker room about all the sexual things he did with his wife. How she loved it when he tied her to the bed or felt her up in public. Roy felt sorry for the woman. Anybody could tell the guy was a liar but to be lied about in such a humiliating way? It made him sick and sped him out of the locker room every time the guy was in there braying.

In his most rootless moments, he felt unknown and unknowable; a phantom moving through incomprehensible landscapes.

Recently, he had taken to driving into downtown Baltimore to wander the streets, just to be anywhere but Dundalk—when he couldn't escape down the Ocean—as far as he could get from his usual frame of reference, from being visible. He'd always been infatuated with the city, with the glimpses of other worlds. He gravitated often to Mulberry Street where he could get a beer at Martick's, a remnant of the Beat scene in Baltimore, without the hassle of being carded. He didn't have a fake ID and looked exactly nineteen.

Even better than Martick's was Sherman's Books, a few blocks up Mulberry, where cantankerous warlord Abe Sherman ruled, terrifying neophytes who made the mistake of admitting they were just browsing. "Buy something or get the hell out!" Abe would shout at some faltering wraith and he wasn't kidding.

Sherman's was a revelation to Roy. Its seemingly endless shelves of books by people he'd only heard of but whose names promised something truly exotic—Céline, Kafka, Ginsburg, Burroughs, Baldwin—thrilled him. Once he'd found them, he read their works voraciously. It was like a library for people on the risky edges of life. He was relieved to have found these writers, like discovering himself moving in pace with an exhilarating, scandalously risky parade.

The other salvation was movies. A monthly film program at Essex Community College had exposed him to foreign films for the first time. The series started with The Seventh Seal and moved on to Rashomon two weeks later. From then on, he couldn't get enough of European and Japanese films, which Baltimore city, with three art house movie theatres, was happy to provide. He felt in on something far beyond the limits of geography and family and old associations. He was a citizen of an utterly new cosmos.

He had also discovered that there were magazines other than Life and The Saturday Evening Post. Magazines about film, like Cahiers du cinéma, and those filled with astonishing writing like The New Yorker or Evergreen Review.

Evergreen Review was truly wild stuff from his perspective: seemingly uncensored, decidedly irreverent. And it was the logical successor to his fascination with Kerouac and other Beat writers. On the New Year's eve sidling blandly into 1962 he'd read On the Road in one sitting and his life hadn't been the same. He longed for the nerve to steal a car and barrel-ass across the country.

He couldn't describe what it was, any of it, except that he had begun to feel an opening out, an awakening, a hunger that school had never given him. Being out of school for the first time in thirteen years had set something loose in him, a sense that there were other realms to know and experience. Evergreen Review and Cahiers du cinéma were talking to each other across the planet in the voices of Henry Miller, Frank O'Hara, Antonioni, Kurasawa. There was something going on that he wanted to be part of, even though he had nothing to add, yet.

This recognition made him wince when he thought of having spent time with Della's brother, Dwight. At the most basic level, Dwight was okay, but he was what one of Roy's favorite high school teachers once called "a happy pig," just content to live and eat and breathe. And that was fine—fine for Dwight and everybody else. But he wanted more, this new Roy, he wanted to experience music, art, theatre, film—all the culture he could, eat it with a greedy spoon.

Away from the drear of the familiar haunts, Roy was starting to feel fiercely alive, as if his brain had abruptly awakened from hibernation. Wandering the streets of downtown Baltimore gave him a sense of being his own man in a way that nothing else ever had. There was something about strolling from Mount Vernon Place to Baltimore Street and back around across Howard or St. Paul, being in the mix of other humans, each in their own bustling privacy, that was magical to him and so unique from the sleepy cicada drone of home.

He liked it best in the early evening when the summer's heat was ghosting up from the sidewalks and the buildings had mostly emptied out into traffic and echoes. He'd walk block after block, absorbing it all. The smell of the streets was a conversation between heated tar, car exhaust and the cool, powdery scent of air conditioned stores and office buildings. The street lights and neon signs coming on bit by bit sent him into a dream state.

There was a sporting goods store he often passed by on his rambles. Some guys were working in the window one evening, changing over the display and that's when Roy first saw the surfboard. It was a luminous green, with a yellow stripe running down the top side.

He stood there so long one of the workers started making goofy faces until Roy had to turn away, laughing and humiliated in the same instant.

From that moment, Roy was on fire to own the surfboard. It wasn't top of the line, not a Hobie, but it was within his financial reach and he wanted it. On his next day off he visited the shop and put money down to hold the board until payday.

His mind raced with the possibilities of what surfing would be like. He'd seen films about surfing, read some magazines. He knew about the culture, about some of the top surfers and the legendary spots around the globe: Rincon, the Oahu Pipeline, Lower Trestles. Day after day, reading, listening to the Beach Boys, Jan and Dean, and songs like "Wipe Out" and "Misrilou," his mind filled with a vision of many oceans criss-crossing one another, pouring out across the globe and he on top of the liquid pyramid, a force fully realized. This was a club he would belong to: surfing and its nonconformist interface with the writers and filmmakers he worshipped.

He was going to do this thing, become a bohemian beach guy, filled with poetry and a camera eye. He'd conquer waves, become a Zen Buddhist, known up and down the coast for writing books, making movies—everything was suddenly possible.

He paid off the board and the next weekend he drove down the Ocean with it secured atop his car with some rope. Roy couldn't wait to get to the beach. He worried about the wind on the Bay Bridge—he could feel the surfboard lifting a little, creating a tiny bit of drag on the car but it came to nothing more than that.

After the bridge, it was sheer frustration. He had to pass through other traffic clumps—Kent Narrows, Easton, Cambridge. Speed up a little, slow down a lot and pray you don't end up on one of the two-lane stretches behind some farmer plodding along with bales of hay piled up on a trailer. Come on, let's go, surf's up!

He pulled up at a traffic light in Salisbury, the last town of any size before reaching Ocean City. He heard a horn beep. He looked across the road to see a kid in baggy shorts and bleached hair leaning against a jeep painted in wild orange swirls. The kid waved and then transformed his hand into the surfer thumb and pinky "hang loose" gesture. Jutting from the back of the jeep was a surf board.

Roy made the hand sign back at the kid, then rolled along with the traffic, smiling. Yeah, man; yes.

The time it took him to get to the spot where he knew the surfers hung out made him almost scream in frustration. Never had the traffic moved so slowly, never had the streets seemed to suck at the wheels of his car like evil tar gods, never had he held his pee so long.

Finally he pulled over near the spot he'd last seen surfers and leapt from the car. Looking around, he hid behind an opened door and released a long stream into the sand. He stripped down to his bathing suit and a t-shirt in the back seat, and applied some zinc oxide to a few still vulnerable spots from the sunburn.

Then it was time. Untying the board, he realized his stomach was quavering with excitement. He grabbed the board wax he'd bought and started walking over the dunes. A second later he turned back to put his wallet away and lock the car, his heart pounding with too much adrenalin to even put in the key.

Once on the shore, he sat a few hundred yards away so he could covertly watch the surfers coming in on the waves. He knew full well that Atlantic waves were picayune compared to the Pacific coast and even those were dwarves compared to Hawaii but at the moment they looked damned big enough to him.

He waxed down the board, trying to avoid getting too much sand mixed in as he hopped around on each side of the shining green surface. He didn't know how much wax to put on for certain so he opted for more rather than less.

Finally, the moment had arrived. He picked up the board and walked to the water's edge. He didn't know if it was okay to ask for help from the gods above so he mumbled, while pretending to wipe his mouth, "Let me do this."

He eased into the cold green water, letting the board take to the surface, plying it along beside him like someone trying to reorient a fish to its element. Soon he was up to his waist where the shore break waves were coming in and he felt the power of the lift on the board as the water surged up into a foaming hump and released toward the shore.

As he got further out, he eased himself up onto the board excited to be starting out—First Man paddling a dugout into the primordial sea.

The sand and wax surface of the board was rougher than he'd realized—his chest would be chafed. He didn't have time to think about it; a wave was coming toward him. He wanted to turn but it was breaking too quickly and the next thing he knew he was nearly on the shore again, holding onto the board in a mad tumble, landing splattered and coughing up water.

He stood up, laughing only to be the first to laugh but no one seemed to be paying any attention to him. Roy started back out. He waited in the shallows and pretended to be retying his swimsuit while watching the guys already in the water, hoping to figure out what they did to get past the breakers. In some cases, if the wave hadn't broken yet they just slipped over the rising water easily, laying prone on the board, pushing down on the nose as the wave rose.

What he hadn't thought about was the buoyancy of the board itself. This wasn't like wading out to body-surf—it was more like trying to sit on a beach ball in a whirlpool.

He watched one guy fight his way through a set of waves, noticing that if a wave was about to break right on top of him, the guy quickly slipped off the board and held onto it from below, then resurfaced once the wave had passed over. Smart, he thought: let the board float; stop fighting the waves.

Determined to get outside the punishing breakers, Roy headed into the deeper water once again, applying what he saw being done. Riding over a gentle swell was easy enough, though he tipped the nose into the water a bit too much, sending up spray into his face.

He barely had time to wipe his eyes when another rising roller bobbed him upwards again, nearly capsizing him. A bit further out, a bigger wave started breaking about six feet in front of him. He dropped into the water, lofted the board with both hands over his head and let the wave crash over the smooth surface.

Surfacing, gagging from having taken in water but about to celebrate, he was abruptly caught in another breaker and once again carried, spinning sideways toward the shore. He dragged the board with him and sat on it at the water's edge, trying to look like a guy just taking five, rather than the half-drowned puppy he felt like.

And so it went for another hour. Roy fighting to get outside of the chop, watching for more hints based on the surfers down the beach, trying to apply what they did and ending up dumped out on the shore each time like some evolutionary reject.

He pulled the board up onto the sand, stuck it nose down in the soft hip of a long dune and sat in its shade. He lit a cigarette and watched as the guys in the water went out and back in, riding their boards like bugs on twigs. He wanted to quit right then and there, leave the stupid board in the sand and walk away.

But that would be idiotic and he knew it too well. This whole year had been about walking away. Giving up on Della: yes, she had given him the boot, more than once, thanks very much. But he hadn't really given up since she left no choice or maybe he did but well, hell, in the end what did it matter: gave up, gave in—what kind of man was that?

Then he complicated things by quitting school and going in to work drunk or sunburned or sick. It was bad enough to be like that since his dad had gotten him the job—the worst of it was that by taking the damn thing he'd capitulated, walked away from doing anything he really wanted to do. He could have found something working somewhere down the Ocean, been here all summer and made out like a king, been able to give over to surfing every day if he wanted, spending time with all the new books and magazines he was in love with, maybe making some new friends worth his time.

Big laugh, he thought; can't see my father going for that option. Much as Roy resented having to accede to his parents, the threat of being told to move out always loomed. He was far from ready for that.

"God damn it all," he said to himself. He jammed his cigarette into the sand and went to the water.

Flinging the board and himself in, he took on the waves again. His collar bone and chest were sanded bright pink and stung in the salt water, his knees were aching knobs from banging onto the board as he tried to get outside or being scraped on the sand and seashell bottom. His shoulders were aching from all the paddling and wrestling the board through the chop.

He didn't care. He was getting out there. It took a few more tries and a lot more bashing but he finally broke past the sets of shore breaks and out into the deeper water. He suppressed the desire to let out a cheer—surfers didn't celebrate minor crap.

He sat astride the board, feeling like a guy in the surfing movies he'd watched. The surface was glassy with drifting colonies of lacy foam. There was a persistent rise and fall beneath him; the water was alive but now it wasn't a deranged beast trying to bash him around but a throbbing thing that had begun to respect him.

He watched for a while as guys down the line paddled furiously to catch a wave, quickly stepping up onto the board and riding along the break. It was magnificent, astounding, like all movies and music and books rolled into one wild release into someplace he could only know by getting there.

Swinging around he began trying to see a wave building toward him. He was ready to take one on, to be flung with all that power toward the shore. There on the crest of a wave, that's where he'd let loose a whoop; that would be the place for it.

He watched a swell rising, turned toward shore and began to paddle. The water began to lift beneath him, his arms became windmills, the board surged forward and the wave was on him.

He felt the water grasp him like a giant hand and start to aim him toward the shore. He paddled hard, harder, then got to a knee—

And fell over, flailing, the board flying out sideways, going along without him, flipping up in the air and finally landing on the sand.

He swam in, body-surfing the next wave that arose—a real beauty he would loved to have caught on the board.

On into the day he went, out to the outside break spots, repeating his furious attempts to get himself onto the board and immediately replicating the scene of splashing sideways into the water like a drunken kangaroo.

After hours of this he finally staggered to his pile of dry clothes, flung the board down beside him and sat dejectedly in the sand. He had no words for this kind of experience. Nothing had ever challenged him like this and he'd simply failed. He wasn't about to cry in public but he certainly felt like bursting loose into a melted beast.

He lit a cigarette, not tasting it, not even feeling it on his lips; it was just something to do in that moment.

"Got another one of those?"

He looked up, squinting into the late afternoon sun. The silhouette was of a girl, but that's all he could make out.

He held the pack out. The girl plopped down on the sand next to him. She was blondish, hair pulled back into a haphazard ponytail. Her skin was that caramel color of what he called "the un-gettable girl." The sort of girl he always saw on the boardwalk in tight white shorts that set off her tan in a way that made his heart seize up. The kind that was inevitably driven away in a Porsche by some smirking frat guy.

And yet this one didn't look like that type at all.

She was wearing a sea-green two-piece bathing suit, the bottom showing slightly above a pair of cut-off jeans. Her belly had a soft little roll to it as she sat there, hunched over, poking her finger in the sand.

"Rough day," she said around an exhalation of smoke.

"Oh, yeah," he said, trying to gun himself up into positive Roy. "But righteous waves, man."

She looked at him a bit sideways. “Yep. Uh-huh.”

He just nodded. Who was he fooling, anyway?

“That your car?”

Roy nodded again. Gee, wow, Mr. Loquacious, he thought. She’s gorgeous and I’m a moron.

“A bit far off the road,” she said. “Hope you don’t get stuck.”

“Me too. I’ll watch that when I come back later.”

“Good plan,” she said, stretching her torso, arms raised, her armpits pale hollows contrasting with the tan.

A moment later, she was standing.

“Take care now” she said, shimmering a wide smile down at him.

“Yeah, hey, you too.”

He watched her walk away.

In his mind he was kicking himself all over the sand. “Righteous,” Jesus Christ on a pogo stick. Why did he always have to be such an idiot?

“Hey,” he said, then trailed off, having nothing to follow it. She waggled her fingers back at him over her caramel shoulder.

He wanted to get up, give chase, but the urge quickly collapsed. His body hurt all over; he was bruised and battered, a little sunburned. All he could manage was to light another cigarette and watch the sway of her hips as she walked along the beach. A clump of guys, boards standing like readied rockets beside them, chatted her up as she passed. Her ponytail arced from side to side as she tossed a few words their way but she kept on walking. It lifted his spirits a little. Guess maybe she really was un-gettable after all, he thought.

Hours later, Roy had gotten a cold shower in a boardwalk hotel outdoor stall, meant for guests to rinse off sand before entering. The cold water didn’t get him completely clean; he was itchy all over from the salt that clung to him. Next time he'd remember to bring soap. Hell, next time maybe he'd have enough cash to get a room someplace.

He had a cheeseburger and fries at Dumser's Dairyland, followed by a banana split to cheer him up, though it didn't work.

Driving back out to the dunes, he began to wonder if he could actually sustain another day of getting the shit kicked out of him by the ocean. He couldn't think very clearly with his stomach bloated and his body feeling like it had gone twelve rounds with Rocky Marciano. Sleep was the next thing, even if it was still light out.

As he pulled near the spot where he'd parked before, taking note of the deeper sand, some movement in the tall grass in the dunes by the roadside caught his eye. Spooked, he hit the brakes and looked around quickly.

Everything seemed okay. He switched off the car and waited, listening to the engine ticking.

His eye caught a flash of something moving behind him, a sudden glimpse in the rearview mirror. He swiveled around, quickly locking his door, hoping that the other doors were already locked. He reached for the keys in the ignition.

A ghostly face erupted at his window, fists pounding alongside it. It was grinning and bobbing, blonde ponytail flipping to and fro.

"Did I scare you?!" She was laughing wildly.

"Hell yeah!" he shouted, trying not to sound as annoyed as he was. He popped the lock and got out of the car. She was standing there, hips tilted, a smile beamed at him.

"I didn't think you'd be back after today. Got your butt kicked out there, buddy."

"Yeah, right; tell me about it."

"Aaah, hell, it ain't no crime bein' a hodad."

"Hey, now, maybe I'm new to this, but not a hodad."

"Yeah, sure," she said. "So, what, you went into town?"

"Dumser's."

"Yeah, I can see chocolate sauce on you. Right there."

He wiped reflexively at his chin.

"Wow," she said, "So you're just a mess from start to finish, huh?"

"Yeah, guess I am. No point being halfway about it."

She smiled and tilted her head sideways, watching him.

He didn't know what to say next. Silence rolled in like a fog.

"Anyway, I'm Roy. Newson. "

"Dina," she said, mocking his serious tone. "Shaw."

Now that they'd swapped more than two sentences, he would bet she was from someplace on the Eastern Shore; her accent was a mix of the flat Maryland sound and the soft lilt of northern Virginia.

He nodded. "Dina." He liked that. The day's warmth was lifting around them from the roadway. The sea grasses were waving in the breeze coming off the water. His skin still itched.

"So you were out here waiting for me?"

"Uhhh, gee no, Mr. Ego. I was waiting for my girlfriend Katy."

"But she hasn't shown."

Dina shrugged.

"So, then, what?"

"I just hitch back into town," she said, all nonchalance. "I know lots of people here; easy to bunk someplace for the night."

"Yeah, I'll bet you bunk all over."

"You have a kind of devious mind there, Newson. Don't use it on me, okay?"

"You're right," he said, "Just being an ass."

"Seems to come easy."

"Years of practice."

"I bet." She shifted her weight to lean on the car. "Anyway, so, you had some day of it," she said, grinning. "You going to sleep out here?"

"Yep."

"You got a blanket? Gets a little chilly past midnight."

"In the trunk."

She nodded. She focused her gaze intently on him in a way she hadn't done before; time stretched.

After what seemed like several lifetimes, she said: "I think Katy definitely flaked on me."

"Oh. That's too bad."

She shrugged.

"I can give you a lift to town if you want," he said.

"I'm cool." She nodded toward the ocean: "Listen, beach patrol won't come by until around eleven. You wanna hang out up in the dunes? Get out your blanket and help see if the moon'll come up later or not?"

God, yes, oh, hell, Jesus, yes-yes-yes, he thought. "Sure," he said, in a half-swallowed voice, trying to maintain his surfer cool.

"All right, then," she said.

They found a great spot, where the sea grass made a semi-circular space, and plunked down to watch the ocean change colors as the sun lowered down behind them.

Anxiety motoring his mouth, Roy asked her question after question. He was thrilled to find out that she was an art major at Salisbury State College and as intrigued by film and everything artistic as he was. They talked excitedly about what each had discovered in the passing year, laughing wildly when both named Jules and Jim as their favorite foreign film so far. Dina's sky seemed to be opening as widely as his in so many ways it staggered him.

Time slipped by and Roy began to relax; the sky turned the color of the ocean and the light began its fade. He let out a long sigh as his aching body began to unknot. She smiled, reached for his hand and pulled them together for a kiss.

Hours later, the moon most definitely up, they were reluctantly evacuating the dunes; sand fleas and other bugs had come out to feast. They went to his car and got in.

"I like your board rack," she teased, pulling on the rope.

"No expense too great, 'mayum,'" he responded, mocking her accent.

"Oh, quit it, you can't do it; I don't talk like that."

"I 'cain't'?"

She bopped him the shoulder.

"Ow," Roy said. "So, when does Salisbury State go back to classes?"

"Not 'til after Labor Day, thank god. Summer of '64 is rollin' along way too fast. How 'bout you?"

Good question, he thought; if I went back now, I could maybe get my associate's in '66. But it didn't feel real somehow; not doable—not him, somehow. "They go back the same time as you. I just don't know if I'm going back. Yet."

"Well, either you do or you don't."

"Wow, what is that: Kierkegaard?"

"Nope. Gamma Shaw. Wisest old bird in any nest."

"Well, okay for Gamma," he said, mocking the term.

Dina smiled wanly. "My Gamma is the one who talked my old man into letting me major in fine art. He was like, 'Dina Leigh' you gotta go inta bidness,' but she wasn't havin' it. She's the one payin' for it, so that just shut his trap."

"Wow: 'Dina Lee.' Love it. L-E-E—like Robert E.?"

"No, dopey. L-E-I-G-H. It's just pronounced Lee. My middle name is after Vivian Leigh."

"Ah, well, same war."

"What a goofy guy you are."

She leaned over until her head came to rest on his shoulder. Roy suddenly found it difficult to get a full breath. He lit cigarettes for them and they rested quietly, taken with the night.

They drifted off to sleep then awoke again when he had a sudden cramp and lurched up to ease it.

"Shit, sorry."

"No biggie," she said, her voice sleep-heavy.

They shifted around into a different tangle. Her body against his so warm; it felt natural.

"Maybe you can tell me a good place for breakfast tomorrow."

She spoke through a long yawn. "Well, maybe up near Rehoboth; otherwise down here it's all greasy spoons, knives and forks."

"Then we'll try it."

"Sure. I work up there, anyhow, at 'Mel's Shell Shop,' so you can take me after we eat. Pick me up later on. If you want."

If I want. He wanted to do a victory dance.

"Sounds great," he said, the essence of cool.

He began to stroke her back, feeling his way up her spine. He loved the silky feel of her skin and fell to musing about what making love with her would be like if he could be that lucky.

"Oh, hey, baby," she said into his chest. "Let me just sleep a while. I was out on that beach all day."

He stopped stroking and allowed his hand to come to rest. "Okay, Dina Leigh."

Roy closed his eyes. He replayed the time they'd spent earlier on the blanket, back in the dunes. Kissing her had been like kissing for the first time, slow and soft and long. Different from Della in almost every way. He whispered "Baby," smiled into the dark, then drifted out.

Some time later, he had no idea how long, he pitched up in the seat: something was dripping on his shoulder. He sat up, fumbling wildly for his watch on the dashboard, knocking it skittering before finally grabbing hold. It was three a.m.

He didn't know where he was or what was making him wet and cold. He clicked his lighter open and saw water dripping down from the surfboard rope. And then it sunk in: rain was tapping on the roof. Fucking rain! Again?!?

Oh, god, not another wet weekend down the Ocean; was this some kind of curse or—

He froze. She was gone.

"What the hell? Dina? Hey?"

He looked in the back seat, on the floor in back, on the floor in front. Nothing.

"Dina!" he shouted rolling down the window an inch, rain splattering in. "DINA!"

The only response was the heavy splatter on the car roof. He lurched from side to side on the seat, trying to see if she was out there. Nothing, just gray shadows falling as water.

He rolled the window closed again and climbed over into the back seat to get away from the dripping. He wasn't worried about the front seat—it was some kind of cheap fake leather that could be dried in about five seconds—but where was Dina?

He clutched the blanket to his chest, fear rocketing through him. Was she gone? What had happened? He was exhausted, couldn't think.

He tossed the blanket aside, ready to jump out to look for her, just as the passenger door burst open and Dina piled in. She knelt on the front seat and shook herself like a wet dog. "Jesus Smith, share that blanket, boy, I am turnin' blue!"

She joined him on the back seat, snuggling into him, as close a spoon as she could manage, backside against his belly, her body in tremors. Her hair was wet, clothes, too. He didn't care.

"God, Dina. Where'd you go?"

"I had to pee! Did you want me to do it in the car?"

"Didn't you hear me call you?"

"I hollered back!"

"Oh. Didn't hear you."

“No more than you heard me get out—you sleep like the dead. You are a bird,” she said with a laugh, and pecked him on the forehead. “No lie.”

They were quiet for a moment; her body had ceased trembling. Holding her felt perfect. The rain on the roof, the steady drip on the front seat—everything perfect.

“You got a leak,” she said, finally.

“Yeah. My high-price surfboard rack needs a tune-up.”

“Seems so. We’ll take it to the special rope-fixin’ shop after breakfast.”

She eased her body around to face him now, pulling them tightly together. She put her nose alongside his, her breath tickling his cheek.

“Surfer Girl” floated into his mind. He gave her a quick squeeze.

“Yup,” he said through a yawn,“after breakfast.”

4

BREATHING

Roy was in love.

Nothing he'd experienced before could have prepared him for this. Everything was Dina. The sky was Dina's eyes, the ocean her smile. It was as if someone had removed blinders from him and there was a horizon again.

It made him crazy that none of his best high school friends were still around so he could tell them about her. Bore them to dirt telling them about her. Bring her around, let them see for themselves.

Even more than that he wanted to run into Della someplace with Dina on his arm. He wouldn't say anything, just gaze in her direction, maybe pity her a little. Ohhh, dear Della, he'd think, poor thing.

He could tell his parents, of course, but they'd find some way to make it less, turn it to shit. Tell him it was just a crush, ask him a million questions with the sole agenda of proving she wasn't worthy, talk about what it would be like once she was back in school. He could hear it coming: "Do you have any idea how hard it is to have a long-distance relationship?" He didn't need it.

Dina, Dina, Dina; she was all he could think about. He caught hell a few times for being in a dreamy state at work. In a way it came natural; the job was so boring.

What he did was inspect huge steel rollers—like enormous versions of rolling pins. Long sheets of steel in massive coils—like scrolls of toilet paper but a zillion times bigger and heavier—were passed between the steel rollers to be made thinner, smoother or even textured for various purposes. He carried around a machine called a profilometer that worked by running a needle similar to the kind found on a record player across the surface of the finished coil. It measured the level of smoothness or roughness of the rolled steel. Once the machine had done its work he marked the roll with the specific readings and went on to the next.

That was it; a trained chimp could have done the job. Probably better.

It was a good idea to stay sharp, though. It was a steel mill. Things blew up now and then. The coiled sheets of steel were run through the rollers at high speeds—walls were gouged in places from flying shrapnel. There was also the chance that he could get run over by the massive machines that carried the coils from point to point, moving aggressively like hell-bent dinosaurs. Everywhere he looked there were signs exhorting safety, including the unnerving one that stated "No Accidents for 41 Days in 1964," with the number 41 entered in chalk over the erased "40." It seemed to Roy that more days going by was less something to brag about than a steady decline in odds.

And what had happened 42 days back? He shuddered to think about it based on stories he'd heard from his father. How coils of steel would break without warning. How some guy had fallen into one of the huge cauldrons of molten steel on the far side of the plant last year. "Nothing left of him at all," his dad said.

He was working one morning, lost in a reverie of him and Dina snuggled in the dunes, wrapped in the blanket, wrapped in each other, when a shadow streaked into his peripheral vision. He was eight feet above the floor, working through a pyramid of rolls.

Some instinct told him to fall flat and he did, like he'd been shot, his breath shooting out of him.

He looked up from where he'd dropped to see a huge coupling sweeping directly across where he'd just been standing. He could have been badly injured, maybe killed. "No Accidents for 1 Days in 1964," the sign would read the day after tomorrow.

He lay on his back for a moment, looking up to high above where the crane was at work, moving back and forth on rails.

A foreman checked on him. Roy assured him he was fine but for a few bruises.

"Yeah, fine this time, bub," the foreman said. "You gotta be wise to where that crane is; he can only see so much of what's below him. That coupling weighs three hundred pounds easy—you're a lucky pup."

Arf, Roy said in his mind, nodding.

He went back to work but the incident troubled him. When he talked to Dina that night on the phone he asked if she believed in signs.

"Sure," she said, a smile in her voice, "Stop signs, for rent signs, no trespassing."

"Very cute. No, I mean, maybe this is telling me to get out of the mill."

"And go back to school?"

"Yeah, maybe that," he said, not altogether certain.

"Something to think about."

"Yeah, it is."

"This is good, Roy; really."

They chatted for a few minutes, then hung up regretfully, mindful of the cost of the call. He was paying room and board to his parents—their idea of teaching him all about the real world—including his part of the phone bill. He didn't mind but that money could be used for something down the Ocean, now that he was going there every weekend. Something, oh, like a motel room, he thought and drifted into a movie of Dina and the room and a bed: muted colors, slow-motion—violins maybe; why not?

He sat in the kitchen, lost in the images. Things had moved fast since the whole July 4th debacle and the confrontation with Della on the street in Dundalk.

He couldn't believe his luck with meeting Dina. They'd spent the rest of the first weekend together, hanging out in his car, laughing their way up and down the boardwalk while the rain idled overhead. She called in sick to the shell shop, unwilling to part with him.

The sun had finally bloomed on Sunday afternoon. They slipped out to their spot in the dunes, grateful to be able to stretch out fully on the blanket after being in the car so much of the time. The sand was rain drop dimpled. The scent of the ocean drenched everything.

"Are you going to try to surf again before you have to go?" she asked as they watched a phalanx of clouds scudding past.

"Doubt it. I still feel like I've been kicked by a bunch of mules."

"Makes sense." She sat up and moved sand around to create a pillow ridge for their heads. In a few moments they were sound asleep.

They woke in the dark and snuggled into one another again, her bottom against him. Roy had to shift his lower body away after a few moments.

"Sorry," he said. A flush of embarrassment broke over him like a wave.

She didn't answer. They lay very still. He wanted her to touch him. His heart was pounding and he considered slipping his hand around to her breast. Seconds slid past; they were motionless. Scenarios flitted through his mind and he wished he'd had experience with girls beyond groping torment. He just didn't know what to do.

Dina sat up after a few moments and leaned over to kiss him. He moved to respond strongly but she held back slightly, making only the barest contact with her lips to his, softly, sticking slightly, her tongue touching his, light as air. It was hard for him to get a full breath.

Being kissed by Dina was so special, meaningful, full of promise, though he had no idea as to what. He didn't care. He thought: let it go on and on.

Finally she pulled back, smiling into his eyes with hers, gripping his hair and rubbing her forehead against his.

"Come on, hodad, you can drive me to Salisbury in a while and then get home to sleep some before your shift in the morning."

"Yeah, 'git' home," he said, grinning broadly.

She laughed. "Now, you just quit that out," she said, putting on a hick accent, "'Fore my daddy come and whup you good."

"Yessum."

They settled back into their beach bed, smiling to themselves. After a moment, she turned on her side and began asking him questions that went beyond playful pillow talk. She wanted to know about Della—know more about the relationship, how they met, what happened with the break-up. He told her selected details, carefully avoided getting into the night when Della got overheated as well as the encounter by the Arundel in Dundalk. Dina smiled and listened, her eyes on his throughout. Her forehead wrinkled a bit when he went into a merciless description of Dwight's shortcomings, so he tried to backpedal a bit and say a few nicer things. He was afraid of her judgment, he knew, and tried to paint an acceptable picture of himself.

Dina prodded him for details about his other girlfriends, his buddies, school and anything else she could think of until he began to feel like she wanted to be his biographer and said so.

"Don't forget to mention the log cabin I was born in," he added, laughing.

"Hey now, you oughta know this about girls by now—curious as cats."

"Mrrrow," he replied.

She made a playful claw and hissed at him.

The following weekend he picked her up in the late afternoon after her shift at the shell shop in Rehoboth Beach.

She came out of the shop smiling hugely at him, looking sweet in her cut-off jeans and an oversized denim shirt tied off at the waist. He groped for words that would describe what he saw as she walked toward the car. Beauty in motion? Every painting of an extraordinary woman? The most perfect Dina in the world? He caught his dopey lovesick expression in the mirror and grinned back at it.

She climbed in and gave him a quick peck on the cheek. He was disappointed and it showed.

“Sorry, Mel’s a big snoop. And a pervert, I swear. One more ‘accidental’ bump into me and I’m going to flatten him. I owe you a better kiss than that.”

“Yeah, I’d say so.”

She laughed and tickled him under the arm.

They drove back down to Ocean City, chattering away. He pulled to the side of the road for the promised kiss. They lingered a long while, touching their faces together, breathing each other’s breaths.

“I’m thinking of getting a room,” he said when they finally broke apart.

“Is that like getting the flu?”

“Depends.”

“On?”

He was about to tell her his movie of the room, but was suddenly too nervous to say anything.

“On how crappy the room is,” he said, finally, with a small laugh.

“Well, as it happens, my friend Cassie is away this weekend and I have her key. If you can work with semi-crappy, this might do it. And for free.”

“Yeah, free semi-crappy would do just fine.”

His heart started the familiar rush again. Was this; could, would this be IT, finally?

“Well, okay, then,” she said.

They decided to eat first. He was glad. The room thing suddenly felt like something ticking. He wanted to be alone with Dina; wanted to make love with her but nothing was certain. It only took one wrong move for a girl to send a guy packing. In that aspect he had plenty of experience. And regrets.

The trouble was there was no way of knowing how a girl would react, so the only choice was to try to ease forward, base by base, seeing how far you could go. There were no rules, no guidebook. And girls were stronger than they looked if you went over the line, bending your hand back or pulling two fingers apart like a wishbone. Many were walking rubberized fortresses with immovable girdles and bras that seemed unwilling to unhook. It was maddening.

One girl said to him, on their first date, just as they were settling onto the couch in her parent's basement club room, "I bite tongues, mister—just keep that in mind." He did and beat a hasty exit an hour later when the show they were watching ended, not willing to risk a momentary impulse.

Figuring girls out was impossible, he had decided.

But maybe Dina would be different. Maybe?

Since he wouldn't be paying for a motel they decided to splurge a little and went to Phillips Seafood House. The smells of the food, of the steamed crabs heaped on paper-covered tables, the spices permeating everything, was heady. They inhaled it, breathed it out again, kissed once, lightly, like grownups on a date.

They didn't look like the rest of the clientele. The place was overstuffed with big family groups comprised of screaming kids and pugnacious teenagers, and islands of older people in couples, stiff and splotchy with peeling sunburns or pale as dead fish. Roy and Dina couldn't stop watching—everybody looked so strained and miserable, trying to make this The Best Vacation Ever.

Dina sketched some of the diners on her napkin. He was impressed: she worked in quick, deft strokes, somehow bringing a person up out of the napkin's surface in just seconds.

"My little Rembrandt," he said.

"Hmm," she said. "Maybe Mary Cassatt."

He just grinned. Mary who?

Leaving the restaurant, Roy began to feel apprehensive and a bit giddy. They were going to a place, a room, together, alone.

The apartment was down a street on the bay side. It took Dina a while to open the door, Roy hyperventilating all the while. He busied himself getting the surfboard off the roof of the car, then followed her in.

Dina was turning on lamps. It wasn't exactly the dump he imagined but certainly messy enough. One room served as kitchen and living room. There was a bathroom with bathing suits and lingerie hanging from the shower rod. And a bedroom. He tried not to linger too long at the bedroom door.

They sat down on the lumpy couch. The coffee table was a piece of raw driftwood sitting on some concrete blocks. Overflowing ashtrays were everywhere, vying with an army of stuffed bears for space. They opened some windows to let the place cool down and air out; a light breeze moved through, stirring the ashes a bit, bringing the ancient smell of the ocean with it.

"Man, I am absolutely full," Dina said, finally sitting.

"Me, too; tight as a tick."

"Oh, yuck, what an image."

"I thought you'd like the country cornpone sound of it."

"You better stop treating me like I'm some hick," she said, laughing. "My father owns that tackle shop across from my house and my mom is a school secretary. And we all wear shoes."

"Well, hush my may-olth," he said, diphthonging every syllable to the max.

"I will," she said and kissed him.

"And anyway," she said when they surfaced, "I hear your Baltimore accent all the time. You actually called that one waitress 'hawn,' instead of hon. And you say 'warsh'—'Ah'm gonna warsh ma hands'—that's how you sound."

"I categorically deny it!" he shouted in mock fury, reaching to tickle her.

"It's true!" she guffawed, dodging away from his gouging fingers, "and you say 'Ballmer' for Baltimore and when you were talking about your little town you said 'Dundock' a few times instead of Dundalk. So don't be throwin' stones, mister."

He laughed with delight. "How about I just throw you another kiss?"

He had no idea how long they were in the flow of lips and tongues and breath. Not that he cared. All he knew was the pressure of their mouths together and in his groin. He wanted to fall into her, on her, surround her. Every part of him was in a state of crazy excitement and desire and he could tell she was responding with the same heat. With a sudden impulse he pulled her to him so tightly her breath leapt into his mouth.

She pulled back. She smiled but her eyes were fixed on him in a way that kept him from immediately smiling back. She stood up and reached for his hand. "Let's go for a walk."

"A walk?"

"Yep."

"But—"

"Nope, but me no buts. Sun's going down in a while and you know I like to watch. Goes plunk right into the bay."

He clasped her hand and she pulled him up from the couch. He needed to stay doubled over as they walked out, hoping to hide his erection, even though she surely knew it was there. He turned it into a joke, making elephant noises and swinging his free arm like a trunk.

They walked to the end of a wooden pier. Some guys were fishing there, cast in fiery coronas as the sun lowered toward the horizon line.

Dina and Roy went to the other side of the pier and sat, feet dangling just above the water. She leaned her head on his shoulder as they gazed into the burning streak on the bay and watched the tiny whitecaps sparkling.

After a bit, she shifted, turning her body toward him, her chin on his shoulder, fingers playing with his hair.

“Listen,” she said, quietly.

“To what?”

“To me, doofus.” She took a quick breath. “I want to tell you something.”

“I’m all ears. Elephant, remember?”

“Har-har,” she said tonelessly.

A silence gathered around them.

She shifted again, her forehead pressed against his tricep. He let his smart-ass pose slip away into the darkening water. This was going to be—well, he didn’t know what, but it was certainly something.

“It’s just—you know I really like you.”

“And I feel the same,” he said, softly as he could.

“You were so honest with me about Della and all. I appreciated that, maybe more than you know. I want to be that open for you.”

“Okay,” he said, wondering how she’d feel if she knew how cherry-picked his honesty about Della had been.

“See, back in high school...” She stopped, plucking at his shirt sleeve. He could feel the tension moving through her.

“What—‘back in high school’ what?” he asked in a near-whisper.

She shook her head and leaned away from him. A line of birds rose from the water, wing tips splashing. For a moment as they passed through the setting sun they seemed to burst into flame and then were gone. Roy blinked back the glare and reached for Dina's hand.

"Hey."

"What?" she said, teetering on tears.

"You don't have to say anything."

"Yeah, I know. But I mean I do. Because of stuff."

"Ohhhh," he said, clowning. "Sssstuff."

"Stop."

"Yeah, okay, okay. Look, whatever it is, it's all right. Okay?"

"I don't know."

"I'm saying that. Guaranteeing it."

"You want to put that in writing?" she said, trying to joke a bit.

"Yes. You can write it on my forehead."

She laughed and shot him an appreciative glance.

"Okay," she said, softly. "Just don't hate me."

"Deal."

A minute passed, then another. He watched some dragonflies getting in some last-minute feeding and listened to the lap of the water below against the pylons. The green reek of brackish water and mud flowed into every inhalation.

"Um, so, just listen, Roy. If you look at me I won't be able to tell you."

He nodded and turned to face along the shoreline.

He felt her pull at his sleeve again then knot it in her fist. "Back in high school, I let this guy, get, um, too close. Thought I loved him or something but he wasn't somebody worth loving." She took in a long, shaky breath. "Anyway, I let him."

She tugged on the sleeve.

"Let him, you know?"

Roy nodded again, swallowing hard against what she was saying. He was holding his breath.

"And next day it was all over school because he was a bragging moron. And that was it for my reputation. Guys started coming around my house, calling all hours, touching me in the school hallways—real fuckin' jerks."

Roy blanched. He'd never heard a girl use that word before; hardly ever heard a girl cuss at all, come to that. Never even heard it from guys in mixed company. He struggled to come back to listening to her. A shower of thoughts was falling through him.

"Then it got worse because my period was late," she continued. "I thought, that's it: my life's over. I was so messed up about all of it—couldn't tell my family and thank God didn't have to. I was never so glad to get my time of the month."

Roy winced. He was lost in confusion. Her sudden bluntness was like a series of slaps.

"Friends were keeping their distance—you got no idea what it's like for a girl. Every day was torture. Anyway, it took me from sophomore year until graduation, holding every damned guy at more than arm's length to try to prove myself—no dating, no prom, nothing. Senior year, a couple of other girls got themselves actually knocked up, so I was old news, finally. But it was too late, anyhow."

She moved away and pulled her hair down the sides of her face, hiding for a moment, then brushing it back.

"So, yeah, hey, me and guys have been a non-thing all this time," she said with a bitter laugh. "But now you. I wasn't expecting you. Or anybody. I'm just the girl on the beach, you know? Everybody knows Dina and everybody knows Dina doesn't go with anybody. Most of them probably think I'm some queer old dyke or something. And then, ka-boom, here's you."

"Sorry," he said, pouting out his lower lip, making her laugh.

"Oh, great, so I just, like, totally barfed up my guts here and you can't resist being a jerk, can you?"

"Nope."

"Jerk," she said, punching his shoulder.

"That's me."

"Well, jerk or no, I do like you. I just don't want to have any misunderstanding."

He nodded.

"I'm saying I'm glad we'll be at Cassie's tonight and if that wasn't available, I'd be fine in a motel with you. Because I trust you, Roy."

Oh, no, he thought, here it comes. He fought the urge to interrupt her.

"Maybe something could happen after a while, um, you know, between us, but for now what I mean by trust is I know you won't try to take advantage of me. I know you're a genuinely nice guy. Maybe in time there'll be a different kind of trust, I don't know. I really hope so."

Nice guy? he thought. No, dammit, I'm a raging beast!

"Anyway," she said, "I hope you're okay with this. And if not, then I'll understand. I'm not a tease. I'm just, I don't know, hoping to get past all that old junk."

He didn't know how to respond. But we have a room, he wanted to say; we're going to be in a r-o-o-o-m!

Instead, he ducked his head, nodded, and kissed her on the forehead.

"It's cool, Dina. It really is."

Her eyes suddenly gleamed with tears and in the same instant she laughed. "Oh, hell," she said, glancing quickly back at the fishermen.

Roy watched her, feeling protective. His sense of her had evolved from the un-gettable girl he plotted and campaigned to get, to—a person. That was the word that leapt into his brain: person, as if Dina was no longer an assortment of smarts and prettiness and the unknown body parts he longed for but another, actual being. He watched those thoughts run through his mind with a kind of wonder. Had he only thought of females before now as trophies or, what, just toys? What was this Dina, some kind of sorceress? Was he good enough for this girl? He shook the doubts away and smiled at her again.

He was disappointed, of course, but at least she hadn't gone the "let's be friends" route, the kiss of death.

The sun kept on its journey. Soon the sky took on the twilight shade of bluish purple that always pulled him upward, wanting to float into it. Dina settled against him, pulling his arm around her shoulder, resting her lips on his hand, her breath warm as the night air.

His thoughts chased each other like the dragonflies they were watching. The feeling of protectiveness for her was pushed aside by a sudden rush of new thoughts: jealousy that some other guy had been with her, that she'd allowed him, "let" him, opened up her body to him. It made Roy feel crazy in a way that thrust him into panic. He tried to push it aside, telling himself that it didn't matter, but it did.

His brain was running a slide show: one moment she was his little surfer girl, in the next a high school kid being ostracized and then he saw her naked and wanton with some slavering fiend. He wanted to punch himself to stop the images.

The fishermen packed and left, taunting one another over their paltry catches, their voices wrapped like knobs in their throats around Appalachian accents.

When the sky went cobalt and the odors of the bay began to intensify with frogs calling and insects whizzing by, they rose and went down the street, arms around one another, quiet at first, then doing goofy walks, tripping over their own feet, laughing.

In the apartment, they listened to music, drank some vile chianti that was no better for having been refrigerated, but got a little drunk and danced.

"We're playing house," he shouted over the radio blasting the Beach Boys' "I Get Around."

"Yup," she said.

“And the rent is late.”

“And the ‘lectricity’s cut off.”

“And we don’t give a good god-damn!”

When they fell into bed together, cozy as kittens, it felt normal, even though it was the first time he was sharing a bed with a girl.

It was different in ways he couldn’t explain; not like with Della in his car or the tongue-biter on her couch or other females in a dozen fervid, furtive places.

In a bed, everything was about bed: you slept in it, you could rest up from an illness, you could spoon. You could have sex.

The jealousy demons leapt up in him again but he kicked them aside. What possible difference could any of it make, he thought. The last thing I want is to be like those kids in her school, judging, snubbing her. What kind of person would that make me?

And you could be plain old happily quiet in a bed, he mused, like now, drifting into dreams, laying on your back while she curls against you, breathing softly. And you don’t have to talk about anything that’s messing with your mind, you could just let it float away.

He still wanted her, still felt the thrum of it in his blood. That wasn’t going to stop. But it wouldn’t be like other scenarios, trying to get what he could out of any girl who let him get close, trying to slip inside each layer of defense—an exhausting comedy that had played over and over. No, this was something else: he wasn’t out to get her, or for her to “let” him.

What he wanted was to join with her in some way he didn’t have a name for, exactly. He just knew it had to arrive mutually.

She was starting to fall asleep; he could hear the shift in her breathing. He reached up and turned off the lamp.

The room turned silvery as light from the street filtered in. He turned toward her, knees to knees, and brushed a stray hair away from her face. Her eyes opened; she flashed a tiny smile at him and let her lids fall shut again.

Dina, he thought, and felt his chest relax, letting go of the knots that had gripped him for hours. He wanted to let go of all thinking and simply be there with her, drifting into a welcome dark of sleep, knowing she was right there, so close they were each other's shadows and light.

He inhaled, deep and long, and let it out slowly until he felt emptied of everything except the need to take the next breath and the one after.

5

SOUTH

Roy was stoked.

He was so full of crazy joy and anticipation he could barely sit in the same position in the car for more than ten seconds.

He pounded on the car horn, joining the caterwaul of other drivers who had lost patience with being stuck on the Bay Bridge, though his blasts were celebratory.

The horns were in full throat all around him. When they settled for a few moments, the radios were cranking out rock and roll from the same local station. When “Chapel of Love” came on, it was clearly the female favorite—shrill voices, some wildly off-key, were wailing it like a delirious anthem. Jesus, he thought, is getting “mar-arr-arried” what they really want?

The traffic inched forward, stopped, crept again. Roy really didn’t care; he had plenty of time to pick Dina up from work. And he was going to try the board this weekend, get on it, get up and fly through the space between wave and sky. The board’s tapered front loomed over the windshield, thrust toward what was next.

Ocean joy, Dina joy and joy of joys: he was no longer a virgin.

Every time he thought about it he broke into a smile and let out a private whoop. Finally at 19 he had joined the world of men. All the self-doubts and worries were mere puffs of smoke now.

He wanted to tell someone about it, but how to do that without confessing his long overdue loss of virginity?

He even thought briefly about telling Dina—but of course he couldn’t and wouldn’t.

Not ever, oh no-no-no.

When the day came when they finally made it, he wanted her to believe she was his first. He hadn't confessed his virginity to her. It made him feel like some hayseed farm boy. Besides he was aware that she'd had experience already. Regardless of the outcome, she knew what he hadn't about the great mystery. Until now.

It would be different anyway, he told himself. They would make love. What he'd experienced two nights back was just fucking. Simple, animal, non-relationship, raw sex with no commitment, no getting "mar-arr-arried" and no weeks-long campaign to get to the act or trying to, no back and forth conversations over why or why not, all the tedious stuff removed and down to the sheer simplicity of it: insert Tab A into Slot A; done.

The cars rolled forward a dozen yards now and started to pick up a bit of speed, horns falling quiet. Maybe the cork had finally popped out of the bottleneck.

As he reached the end of the bridge "Rag Doll" by the Four Seasons came thumping on from the collective radios, with its portentous drum opening. Roy chuckled, expecting to hear male voices around him cracking pathetically trying to reach Frankie Valli's falsetto heights. He wasn't disappointed: straining warblers crashed in heaps and waves. He had long since given up trying to match Roy Orbison or Brian Wilson, telling Dina jokingly "I'm too much man to sing that high."

And indeed, now, his body reliving the experience of two nights back, he knew he really was too much man, all man, in fact: a man among men.

Glancing over, he caught the eye of a pretty brunette singing along to her car radio, bouncing on the seat. He gave her a smile, something he would normally be too hesitant to do but he'd come into a new awareness: all women were known and knowable to him now. She returned his smile, then abruptly lurched forward, cutting him off in the lane. Was that flirting? he wondered. Like the girl who took his baseball cap one day and wore it around school for hours or the one in junior high who used to bash him with her purse getting off the school bus. True love back in those days.

He laughed as the brunette continued to bully her way through the lanes, evidently focused on a gas station a ways up. Not flirting, he thought, arching up in his seat to see her now tearing along the shoulder, raising dust: she really needs to pee or something—hope no cops are around.

Roy settled back in his seat again. Traffic moved a few yards, stopped, moved again. He let his eyes go out of focus while he chased the recollection of two days back.

The evening had started without expectation of any kind. He'd driven into Dundalk, curious to see if anybody he knew was hanging around the Arundel corner.

He was leery of running into Della again but what could she do to him now that he had Dina? Go ahead, he thought, yell at me: I'm Della-proof.

Much to his delight, there was Phil Camber, standing in the center of a group of admiring younger guys. Phil, one of his two best buddies through the last two years of high school.

Phil was a very compelling figure. Well over six feet tall with thick dark hair shaped with seeming ease into the perfect pompadour, Phil was a weight lifter with a finely sculpted body. An obvious magnet for girls, he said he'd lost his cherry at fourteen and there was no reason to disbelieve him . Roy always felt more attractive to girls when he was hanging out with Phil and safer around the ever-looming threat of hoodlums in his high school and at the teen center dances. People made way when Phil walked into a room and with good reason: Phil could kick ass when he chose to let loose.

What Roy knew was that Phil was an amicable guy who saw the world with a comic view of human nature.

They'd met in summer school the year after 10th grade. Roy was taking Algebra again, having barely passed, and Phil was in a remedial composition class. There was a long portico at the back of the classroom hallway where the students were allowed to smoke and hang out during breaks. It was a great place to stand—shady, with the air conditioning flowing out of the open hallway doors, wafting a complex teenage stew of perfume, aftershave and armpits, along with the perennial high school scents of pencil shavings, cafeteria odors and chalk dust.

At first Phil and Roy ignored each other, out of male custom. The next day Phil asked to bum a smoke and they fell easily into talking about the bullshit of summer school, cars and sundry other safe topics. When the bell sounded, students started to stream back to the classrooms and Roy witnessed a moment that marked his admiration for Phil indelibly.

Most of the students had gone in already. One girl hung back. Roy had noticed her a few days before—dirty-blondish, with a full, womanly body. As she entered the building, she slid past Phil, who was leaning in the doorway. Roy's eyes bugged out as she swiped her breasts against Phil on the way.

It was such a deliberate act that Roy couldn't discount it as a clumsy moment.

Roy's brain slammed to a halt. He had never seen anything like it. His mouth opened, then closed and opened again. He looked at Phil, who grinned, performed an elaborate shrug and shot his cigarette out into the grass with a practiced flick of his fingers.

After the weekend, Phil confided that he and the girl had made it in her car on Friday night. Roy kowtowed to him, bowing and muttering praise in a made-up language, making Phil choke on his soda.

They were close buddies after that. Roy had already decided by the spring of tenth grade he'd had enough of the grade-grubbing, obsequious kids in the advanced classes. He just wanted to be with regular people who knew school was a pain. He ended up in Social Studies class with Phil. They carried on a lively exchange of notes during every class from then on and hung out on the weekends, drinking and driving around, going to the teen center.

After graduation they lost touch. Roy called a few times, wrote some letters but Phil wasn't the letter writing type. Finally, Phil's mom answered the phone and told Roy that Phil was visiting family in Pennsylvania for the summer, so that was that. But now, here in this surprising summer of '64, there was Camber once again back at their old hang-out, like no time had passed.

"What are you doing here?" Roy asked, as the knot of kids clumped back into the Arundel ice cream parlor.

"Short break from summer sessions. Meant to call you but I actually didn't know if I would get home or not."

"How's U of M treating you?"

"It's okay. Remedial classes are harder than I figured. Dorm life sucks. My roommate's this guy with asthma who picks his zits at night." Phil made a gagging sound.

"Shit. I'd hate that," Roy said with a shudder.

"So, listen, I'm glad I bumped into you. I really was going to call but you know how it gets when I come back. I swear to god my mother's making about twenty different meals right now and expects me to eat them all while I'm here for three days."

"Oh, yeah, poor you."

"Anyway, yeah, so there's a party. John Zucker's."

"Okay."

"But there's supposed to be this girl."

Roy nodded, pretty sure of where this was going.

"O'Donnell Heights, Roy," Phil was saying, lowering his voice to an urgent rumble. "That's the rumor: a bunch of Heights girls."

In their world, neighborhood equalled identity. Sometimes a party-thrower would invite girls from O'Donnell Heights, a low income housing area legendary for uninhibited behavior, to liven parties up. Nobody invited males from the

Heights, though—switchblades and chains might come with those guys.

But Roy knew the likely reality: twenty boys would be lurking around and a half dozen scrawny Heights girls would be practically clinging together in a corner while the home turf girlfriends seethed with unmasked outrage—and nothing would happen. Boozed enough, some guy might make a move, get his face slapped and ten minutes later the Heights flock would be in the wind, thoroughly pissed at the assumption they were easy. Out of frustration somebody would start a fight, the party would break up and Roy would swear off parties built on stupid rumors for life.

Even so, he agreed to pick Phil up at eight. The party was irrelevant—he just wanted to catch up with his old pal. It could be the last chance to visit for a long time if Phil got into the University of Maryland in the fall. Roy hadn't made a ton of friends in high school. The ones he had were the out-of-sight/out-of-mind types. It hadn't taken long after graduation for Roy to realize there was no point in trying to maintain contact with them.

He chuckled as he watched Phil emerge from his house, wearing nice slacks, white shirt, jacket and tie, always looking like the proper young man around his family. If they only knew what a total horny hound he could be, Roy thought with a smirk. Roy was wearing chinos and a button-down shirt.

It only took a few minutes to find an older guy who would get them a bottle. They sat outside the party house, passing the fifth of vodka back and forth, watching other people arriving. It was a mix of Joe College types, like Roy, with their neatly combed side-parts and "Hairs" like Phil, with their greased-up pompadours.

Once inside the basement, what Roy had expected was on full display. There was a clump of Hairs in black t-shirts, cigarette packs rolled up in sleeves, and a mascaraed knot of their girlfriends, with their tight skirts and poison apple lipstick, passing several bottles around. In the corner a smattering of Madras-shirted Joe Colleges had gathered, outnumbered and looking around warily, sharing their own booze.

Six Heights girls were sitting on a couch, practicing the art of indifference. You couldn't miss them. Five were dressed in pastel slacks and ruffled blouses, immovably lacquered hair, faces well-stuccoed over acne, working wads of gum furiously. But the sixth was radically different. She was wearing a white blouse, plaid skirt and saddle shoes, looking as if she'd just come from Mercy High, a Catholic girls' school across town. Guy-world lore was that Catholic school girls were easy pickings from being actively repressed their entire lives, but this girl looked like she was two-thirds nun already.

The party was in motion; music roaring, a few girls dancing together, everybody else talking animatedly and no hostility between the factions so far.

In time the plaid skirt girl moved to stand by a wall, pulling a girlfriend with her, leaving the other four sitting on the couch looking as if they'd prefer to be roasting over a pit. Now and then one of the Hairs would approach the plaid skirt, chatting away for a few minutes and then retreat hastily in flames. This girl was clearly not the "this girl" that Phil had alluded to earlier.

Still, Roy thought, it was worth a shot just to see what Miss Plaid was all about; she'd rebuffed every guy that had approached her so why not become a member of the rejected? After that maybe he could talk Phil into splitting.

"Let's go talk to her," he said.

"Lost cause, man," Phil shot back. Roy could tell that Phil was bored and getting into war mode, thinking about starting up some shit with somebody. Even so, he moved with Roy toward the wall.

"Hey," Phil said, flashing a piano's worth of white teeth.

"Eww," the girl said, "another Hair, get away from me."

Phil gave her a hard look and stepped back. His face had gone very dark at the rejection and Roy knew somebody was going to be bruised and bleeding soon.

"Well, what about me?" Roy asked.

"Oh, no, " she said, "you can stay; Joe College guys are okay! You seem really okay."

Roy's response was instantaneous, coming back with a line he often used as a kind of joke, based on his significant nose: "Yeah, I'm just a good little Jewish boy."

At which the girl screeched, "I love Jews!" and pushed Roy against the wall, her tongue going straight into his mouth, her lower body glued to his. He was pinned there by her, his eyes open and looking around wildly.

Half a dozen guys materialized suddenly. "I'm Jewish, I'm Jewish," they were shouting. The girl paid them no mind; she was busy in Roy's mouth, her legs now straddling one of his. He could taste the whiskey she'd been drinking, Southern Comfort, the sweetness of it mixing with the waxed flower flavor of her lipstick. Ignored, the boys skulked back, resentfully rejoining their little tribes.

"I gotta pee," she said suddenly and broke off, heading for the stairs, towing her girlfriend along with her. She glanced back at Roy once before going out of sight.

"What the hell was that?" Phil asked.

"Man, I don't know. She just kind of went nuts."

"You got it made, Roy," Phil said. "Get upstairs before somebody gets more Jewish than you."

Roy laughed but he still hesitated. He was torn: Dina was filling his mind, her face, the sweetness of her tender kisses, not like this girl with her aardvark tongue—but his body was raging.

He waffled a moment longer, then went up the steps, trying to act nonchalant. He passed through a warren of rooms before coming to the girlfriend standing guard.

"Just don't," she said, her face a knot.

"What? I'm just making sure she's okay."

"Yeah, sure."

"Why don't you mind your own business?" Phil's voice seemed to surf across the top of Roy's head, startling him.

"She's my best friend, come on."

"I don't know what you're all worked up about," Roy said, feeling weaselly even as he spoke.

The door flew open and the girl came out. Her cheeks were flushed pink and her eyes glittered.

"Angela—" the guard girl started.

"I'll be okay," Angela said, her gaze set on Roy. "You got a car there, Jew boy?"

"Yes, yeah, uh, yes I do," Roy bleated.

"And a bottle of somethin'?"

"Oh, yes. Vodka."

"Okay then." She grabbed his hand, nearly pulling him off his feet. She stopped abruptly and turned, noticing Phil following. "Him, too?"

"He's okay. Big Jew from U of M."

"College man? Oh, baby, hell," she said and lurched forward.

They got in his car and Roy pulled away quickly, imagining a raging mob descending on them with pitchforks and torches. He was thinking they'd go to a drive-in place or something, see what was what, but she was immediately trying to work his zipper, her tongue in his ear.

"You're going to make me wreck," he said, trying to dislodge her gently.

"No sweat," she said and slid over the front seat to Phil in the back, throwing herself onto his lap.

"Get going, Roy!" Phil spluttered.

Roy drove as fast as he dared. There was a place he'd gone once with Della, very secluded along a dark back road.

Sounds in the back seat made it seem as if a karate match had broken out; the girl had gone manic and was thrashing around wildly.

Roy turned to tell Phil to keep things cool, but found himself confronted with the girl's naked crotch as she arched and bucked.

"Jesus, Phil, keep her down; we're in traffic."

"I'm tryin', man, I'm tryin'!" came Phil's harried voice an octave above normal. Roy tried to imagine how strong the girl would have to be to give Phil such a rough time—the guy could clean and jerk about 150 pounds like it was nothing.

In a few minutes they were out of traffic, out of streetlight reach and back in a wooded area. Roy parked, trying not to listen to the animal moaning and writhing going on in the back seat.

He got out, feeling disturbed and frightened.

He stood in the dark for a few minutes planning to drive away as soon as Phil was done. The whole thing was too weird. He pictured Dina and knew he had to bail on this craziness.

He heard the door open.

Looking back he was dumbfounded. There was Phil, still in his tie and jacket, white shirt, shoes and socks, but no pants.

"What, uh, what are you—" he stopped, realizing that Phil was making peculiar sounds. Was he crying? Phil crying?

"I drank too fucking much, Roy. I can't do it, can't get it up. God damn it." Phil covered his face.

Roy started to say something but nothing would come to mind that didn't sound completely moronic.

From the car came Angela's voice. "Hey Jew boy, get over here!"

He hesitated, his stomach rolling over. Just leave, he thought. Get Phil in the car and get out of here.

He glanced toward the car. Angela was kneeling on the back seat, pressing her bared breasts against the window.

Rational thought flew from him. He raced toward her, blood pounding in his ears.

This was going to be it, the big IT, the absolute and true it; he had no time left for Phil or Dina or thought.

She dropped back on the seat as he approached. Her eyes still emanated the spooky sparkle he'd noticed before.

She opened her arms to him, her legs parting. He dropped his pants down and let her pull him to her. He fumbled around trying to find his way into her. He'd touched vaginas before but this was a docking maneuver he'd never undertaken. She reached to guide him in. She felt dry to him, unyielding, not what he'd expected; he pushed hard, then much harder—abruptly he was in, enveloped. He nearly cheered.

Moments later it was over. He eased back from her, then leaned in to kiss her lips, realizing he hadn't done so up to that point and feeling now like a complete ox, cluelessly following instinct. As he rocked back onto his knees, he noticed Phil staring through the back window at the girl's body. A vile taste rose in his throat—had Phil had been watching all along?

He eased out of the car. The girl was crooning to herself. Phil rushed past him into the back seat; Roy heard the girl release a long sigh.

He walked a few yards away. He could hear the car rocking on its springs. Looking up, he gazed at the stars hovering above a blurry moon. It smelled like rain.

So, he thought, that was it. That was sex. It felt good but was that it? He didn't know; it just seemed like put it in, thrust a while and done. That couldn't be all, could it?

He didn't want to be disappointed or confused but he was. He hoped it would be different with Dina. It had to be, right? Because this was what everybody made a big deal of all the time. Maybe he hadn't done it right.

Soon Phil was standing next to him, pants back on.

"We ought to get her back to the party," he said.

“Yeah,” Roy said. “I think we need to drop her off near the party, if you know what I mean.”

“Um, yeah, those other guys’ll be pretty pissed off.”

They drove back in silence. The girl sat against the back door, motionless like a life-sized doll, vaguely smiling. The car had filled with her scent, acrid and palpable. When they were a block away, he stopped. Phil got out and opened the back door. Roy couldn’t hear what he said to her but after a moment she passed by the car, moving languidly toward the party house, the bottle of vodka dangling from her hand.

She stopped, looking back at them. “I love Jew boys,” she said and drifted away.

Roy turned the car around and drove away quickly. They ended up at a smokey burger joint on Pulaski highway, full of night owls scowling into their plates, everybody minding their own damn business.

Roy was starting to feel very mixed about what they’d done but Phil was very animated, laughing as he recounted trying to keep Angela from kicking out the rear window. He realized that Phil had no sense of conflict about what had happened and maybe he shouldn’t either.

He felt bad for Angela, though, and unable to understand what her world was like. He justified it all in his mind: she grabbed me, practically tore my clothes off, so it’s not like I took advantage. Besides, he thought, I got laid. I just got laid for the first time and that’s really something. Tab A, Slot A, dammit; screw the rest of it.

To celebrate, Roy bought them each a slice of coconut cream pie. It tasted like soap.

When he woke the next morning he was surprised to find an inch-long abrasion on the shaft of his penis he hadn’t noticed before going to bed. He recalled how dry she’d been, how difficult to penetrate her. The wound hadn’t scabbed over fully—it really stung when he probed the area.

Jesus, he thought, how did this happen? Please tell me this isn't some disease from her. That would end things with Dina like a shot.

Blaring car horns pulled him back into the traffic jam off the Bay Bridge. Angela vanished like a popped bubble.

The line of cars were finally getting up to speed. Roy turned his radio up as "Can't Buy Me Love" came blasting on.

He slipped into a funk in spite of the upbeat music. He had to admit he didn't like himself very much about the whole Angela thing, that he really hadn't given much thought to her at all. Was she okay, did she go with other guys at the party? He guessed from the hostility of her girlfriend that Angela had probably done this before. Why go to a party then? Hell, why go with Angela to a party if she wasn't really going to protect her?

He shook his head to clear it. What's done is done, he told himself; let it go and say never again. Only one woman in this world: Dina.

When he pulled up to Mel's Shell Shop, he was thrilled as always to see Dina emerging from the gloom of the little store and into the sunlight. Nothing else meant more to him.

He drove them to their favorite spot on the beach. Both had their bathing suits on already; hers was new to him, a deep blue one-piece that showed her body off. He hoped she'd bought it with him in mind.

He got the board off the rooftop and walked hand in hand with her through the dunes and sea grass. They were chatting about everything that had happened during the week with their jobs and friends. As Dina sat down on the sand, her legs parted and the hollow of her inner thigh flashed white above her tan. The memory of Angela's exposed lower body sliced through his gut. He clenched his eyes shut until the vision passed. Turning to look at Dina, he summonsed a smile.

"Here goes nothin'," he said.

Board waxed, face set and determined, he walked into the ocean, immediately feeling the sting of salt water on the open sore inside his trunks. He dove in quickly to hide his embarrassment.

Dina followed him and swam out a few yards. Roy collected the board, more confident now. He got past the tricky rollers easily this time, having rehearsed it in his mind for days. When he got into open water he sat up on the board, straddling it, watching out to sea for a decent size wave to catch.

Something nipped his toe; he yelped and nearly capsized. Dina's head bobbed up out of the water, a broad smile on her face.

"Shark got ya," she said, laughing.

"Shark's going to get a spanking."

"Oh, yeah, by you and what army?"

"You'll see," he said, reaching to caress the top of her head.

"You ready for this, hodad?"

"Ain't no hodad, lady; me big surf master."

She smiled again. "Then you go get 'em." She turned and swam toward shore, smoothly carving through the water. He waited until she was emerging out of the chop before he turned again to look out for something building for a ride.

Down the beach, the other surfers were in their usual place. Maybe I'll go hang out there once I get this going a bit. Yeah, I'm going to be in that whole scene, Dina by my side, little surfer girl, damn straight.

The sun was pelting down. He eased off the board to cool off, then back on. Scanning the horizon, he saw the swell he had been hoping for, building in a fat hump that looked as if some massive sea creature was on its way.

He turned and began to paddle easily, letting the rise come to him bit by bit. When he felt the inevitability of the wave his arms began to windmill, pushing him faster. The wave formed beneath him, he could feel the lift, the power of it, now accelerating with him in mutual force.

The wave began to crest.

He pushed himself up, not fully trusting it, taking a wide stink bug stance, feeling the phenomenal energy of the water peaking and continuing to rise until he thought he'd be flung into the sky. He was surfing!

He tried to turn into the curl, to ride it along as far as he could but lost his balance.

The board shot out from beneath him straight into the air like a missile. He lost sight of it as he plummeted into the water, landing in the still-breaking wave and being rolled by it helpless as a rag doll, his back scraped by the sea floor debris.

Water invaded his mouth and eyes and ears; he tried to scramble to a standing position but nothing could tell him which way was up. Finally the wave opened its fist and he came to rest on his knees, shaken, his head ballooned with salt-sharp ocean slurry.

It took a few moments before he could stand. Some seagulls flew over him, their cries mocking him. Yeah, go ahead and laugh, he thought.

He began wading toward the shore. A wave hit him from behind, propelling him into a stagger. Just as he found his balance the powerful undertow nearly pulled his feet out from under him. This ocean is trying to kill me, he thought, with a wry grin.

He went slowly, struggling with shaky knees, trying to pop the water out of his ears.

Dina was sitting at the water's edge. Her smile seemed brittle. He didn't know what to make of it until he saw that she'd pulled his board next to her on the sand.

The nose was broken off.

He couldn't understand the things that flashed through his brain in the instant when he saw the board: Angela's bare breasts at the car window, Phil staring at them on the back seat. The salt-burning sore spot leapt into flame as he stood there—he wanted to adjust himself but couldn't do it in front of Dina.

The broken board came into focus again. He covered his eyes, trying to stave the tide of emotions. This is what I get for doing what I did.

Dizzy, he slumped down on the other side of the board, not willing to be embraced by Dina.

"God almighty," he said.

"I'm sorry, baby," she said. "It flew straight up and came straight down in the shallows. Kind of stuck there for a bit and then fell over."

He nodded.

He reached for the board, pulling it around to where he could see the damage. A foot-long part of the front end was broken off. He picked up the piece and fitted it to the break point; it matched seamlessly.

"You can put it together again, I bet," Dina said softly.

"Yeah, maybe. I don't know."

A shadow fell on the board. Roy looked up to see a guy standing there, shaggy blond, a board under his arm, like some illustration from a surfer magazine.

"That's bad," the guy said.

"No kidding," Roy shot back, pissed at everything in the universe.

"He could fix it, though, right?" Dina asked.

"Doubt it."

"What?" Roy said, voice going high as Frankie Valli's.

"Ain't just a bad break. It's a bad board. That's just styrofoam in there and they just covered it with some kinda lacquer insteada fiber glass. Ain't a real board, more a toy for a lake or someplace. Too light for a real wave. Your boyfriend got took, Dina."

And with that, he loped down the beach toward the surfer spot. Roy wanted to punch the guy's lights out.

He felt as if his entire body was crumbling into the sand where he sat.

He didn't know what to say or think. He knew the board hadn't cost near as much as the boards he saw in the magazines, but he figured those were boards for California, Hawaii, and needed to be more rugged. And he had wanted it. Wanted that board in a desperate way, so he never asked about what it was, if it was the real thing. He was shouting in his head: Idiot, idiot, stupid jerk asshole, idiot!

Dina was crouched behind him now, rubbing his back gently, blowing softly on the shell scrapes, but he wasn't there.

He was lost in a sun-blasted world, foundered by a comet shower of every failure that wanted to mock him: Della storming away in Dundalk, Dwight's broken-toothed grin, the scent that emanated from Angela's body—an odor he could still smell, a sick sour reek that made him retch.

Everything had gone south. He touched his belly, feeling a welt announce itself with a bright stinging. The sore spot on his penis had stopped hurting but was itching now. Roy shook his head in exasperation.

They sat in silence for a long while. Gulls lofted and wavered overhead, surfers shouted and laughed, the ocean crashed on the shore.

Some while later they were sitting side by side in a booth. He didn't even know what restaurant it was, just some burger joint; didn't matter. Dina was trying to ease him out of his mood, with little success. Some kid with orange hair and a face full of zits brought their food, thumping across the floor with a limp. There was a cast on his foot with writing all over it.

"Enjoy," he said, half-heartedly, then clomped away.

"Yeah, thanks," Roy responded in the same tone, thinking that at least he wasn't that poor guy, though it didn't much lift his spirits.

Dina picked up a french fry and offered it to him. He didn't want it, didn't want anything but opened his mouth anyway. Her empathy made him uncomfortable. She'd already told him about ten times how sorry she was about the board. How could he face where the true blame was?

They ate in silence for a few minutes.

"You know what I heard?" she said, with a sudden brightness.

He shrugged.

"A Hard Day's Night opened in London last week. People went nuts for it."

"Cool."

"Yes, cool, mister. It'll be coming here! Well, not here, but Baltimore for sure. We could see it together."

"That would be nice."

"'Nice.' 'Cool.' Where'd you learn such big words?"

"Dina—"

"Nope, nope, no sir. This is the Beatles. You gotta know how amazing this is going to be, right? I mean, okay, Ed Sullivan and all so we got to see them—I mean, did you watch?"

"Yes, of course; everybody did."

"Right? But this is a movie. Big screen! The four of them, close enough to touch, bigger than your Aunt Fanny's fanny."

"I haven't got an Aunt Fanny."

"You just think you don't."

"Dina, come on—"

"Nope, nope, we're going to pep up here, buddy. Talk and such." She thought for a moment. "Okay, who's your fave, tell me that. Come on, I know you got one."

He let out a big sigh, just wanting to sulk and be pissed off about everything but she was relentless.

"All right, already: it's John. John is the cool guy, best voice and all."

"Hmm," she said. "Yeah, he's really good. You know who I like best? Ringo."

“Ringo!??” He glanced around, not meaning to have raised his voice.

“Yes, Ringo. He’s cute. He’s got a significant honker like somebody I know,” she said and tweaked his nose, “and he looks like a sad puppy.”

“Nobody likes Ringo best, Dina; he’s just the drummer.”

“I don’t care.”

“Christ: Ringo; that’s just ridiculous.”

“Maybe so, but I know what I like and I like what I like,” she said and took a big bite out her sandwich. She chewed for a moment, then nudged him. When he turned to look at her, she opened her mouth wide to display her food.

“Yuck!”

“Gotcha.”

“Yeah, you got me, just like your shark did,” he said, finally raising a pale laugh.

They smiled into each other. She leaned against him and they went on eating, only occasionally chatting but mostly back on the same planet.

As the sun was easing into the horizon they drove to a place Dina knew where people dumped cast-off junk.

“What you need is a farewell ritual,” she’d said at the restaurant.

“Yeah,” he said. “Let’s get some lighter fluid and—“

“Whoa,” she said with a laugh. “Let’s not bring the fire department in on this. Something a little less vivid, maybe.”

For the ceremony they lit half a dozen cigarettes and poked them into holes in the rusted sheet metal fence that partially surrounded the dump, watching the smoke rise into the lavender evening air. They stood the broken surfboard and the chunk in the well of an old-time wringer washing machine. They stood in silence for a while, then walked slowly to his car.

The fading light revealed some smears on the car’s rear window, one of which looked like a footprint. A chill went through him as he realized he'd never checked the back seat for any tell-tale leavings.

"You can always buy another board," she was saying, as they drove away.

"Nah," he said, shaking off his guilty thoughts. "I think maybe being a surfer isn't really for me."

"Really? Just like that?"

"No, not just like that. I didn't even want to try getting on it last weekend, if you recall. It was—I don't know—just a thing for a minute, you know?"

"Sure, I get you. Guess you got no reason to come back down the Ocean now, though, huh."

"Nope."

"Yep, that's too bad."

"Of course," he drawled, "if I had, like, I don't know, a girlfriend or something."

"Yeah, that could be motivational."

"Could be. Know any girls around here?"

She punched his shoulder, then pressed her face into it. The ache in his chest eased.

They were staying at yet another place belonging to one of her friends. Roy was really getting to know the nitty-gritty life of Ocean City.

She sketched quick portraits of him for a while until he got tired of sitting still. They listened to music, danced, watched a little TV, then decided to "hit the hay," as Dina liked to call it.

In bed, they held hands and gazed at reflections on the ceiling from passing traffic. This place was closer to the boardwalk than the others had been. They could hear conversations of passers-by, the mumble of cars cruising past.

She moved to rest her head on his shoulder, pulling his arm under her neck for support. He was still bummed about the board, lost in his brain with regrets about buying it, losing it. Just when he'd let those thoughts go, memories of the party would surface again. His body felt tense, alien.

“I think I’m going to have to cheer you up some more, maybe even a whole lot more,” she said. She finger-walked down his chest and kept going until leaping abruptly onto his boxer shorts.

He jolted away, startled. She’d never touched him before and she’d hit directly on the sore spot.

Dina jerked her hand back. “Damn, buddy, didn’t mean to scare you,” she twanged as he sat up against the backboard.

“You didn’t. You surprised me but it’s okay.”

“You sure? You really jumped. Guess I shoulda warned you.”

“It’s okay, really.” Mice were racing around in his head, unsettling him. A flash of Angela’s exposed body, her pale legs, matted pubic hair; the smell.

He fell silent. Moments passed. Dina sat still, watching him apprehensively.

“Do you,” he started, faltered, went on. “Do you think we could still wait?”

“Wait?”

“Yeah. Just— I don’t know. You’ve wanted to wait and that’s been fine. I mean, I totally understood.”

“Yes and I’ve been glad about that, Roy.”

“But maybe it’s me that’s not ready now or something. Would that be okay? I mean, is that weird? Shit, that’s weird, that’s really weird. I’m sorry.” He wanted to shout down the ceiling around them.

“Stop. No, it’s not weird.”

“Are you sure? I mean, guys are supposed to be, like, all aggressive I guess but I just—“

“You aren’t ‘guys,’ you’re Roy and I don’t want you to be anybody else.”

“That’s really good. I mean, so long as you’re seriously okay about it.”

“Are you kidding?” she asked, smiling.

“What do you mean?”

"You know how many girls would like to meet a guy who could think with something other than his pecker?"

"Ummm—"

"A whole bunch, believe me. You are really something."

Yes I am, he thought, but what kind of something?

She turned to gaze more directly into his eyes. Something slipped into the room and held them together in mutual gaze, not quite able to breathe.

Dina spoke first.

"I love you, Roy."

Roy smiled widely. This was the first time she'd said it to him. His lungs took in air.

"I love you, too, Dina; I really and truly do." He was amazed at saying it. How it just came right out of him. Had he ever said it to a girl before? He'd "really liked" quite a few, but to say that word? Never. But there it was, as real as anything.

Dina pulled his hand to her lips and kissed it.

"Good, so we wait. I don't mind and that's a fact, okay? I'm all yours when you're ready. Cool by you?"

"Yes."

"There you go then." She bugled a long wet raspberry on the back of his hand, easing the hovering air around them. They fell back, laughing.

She found his face, stroked it, kissed him soft and sticky many times, then once, fiercely. She curled into him again, easing her leg lightly over his shin.

In a few minutes her breathing changed to the sleep rhythm he was already so familiar with.

He watched the play of lights move across the ceiling and walls for a long while, rooted by her warmth. People continued to drift by, their chatty voices indistinct—lighthearted end-of-the-day word songs.

His thoughts circled. The sore spot began to sting and itch again, as if he needed a reminder that they could be making love right then.

You owe her the truth, he thought, as he began drifting off. And immediately knew it was a terrible idea—she'd kill him and he would deserve it.

Roy, man, he thought: you are one stupid idiot.

6

ELSEWHERE

Roy was seriously upset. And very worried.

He had no idea how long he'd stood there with the phone in his hand, the connection dead—waiting for something to make sense.

When he'd answered the phone, it was Phil Camber. Phil's "Hey" sounded so hollow, Roy kept silent until Phil spoke again.

"We got a nail, buddy."

A moment passed as Roy waited. Was there more? What was a nail?

"The clap," Phil said.

Finally, Roy: "Ummm, what?"

"Yeah, that girl at the party?"

"Angela?"

"Yeah, who else? Fucking Angela. She gave us a dose."

"I don't know what you're talking about."

"You haven't been peeing fire?"

"Oh, well, yeah, a little."

"Dripping weird stuff?"

"Yeah, but I just figured it wasn't anything." He didn't want to mention the sore spot, which had mostly healed.

"Well, it ain't anything, it's something. Gonorrhea, my doctor said. You need to go get checked out."

"Shit."

"Yeah, exactly. Sorry, man, gotta go—my ride to school's here. See ya."

"Hey, but—"

But Phil was no longer on the line.

Roy was bewildered. "Why me?" was his first thought but then it was really "Why us?" and behind that the recognition that neither had cared about anything except having Angela.

Roy was like all guys his age, with a condom aging in his wallet —but to think to use it in the crazy heat of the moment? And anyway, until it happened, the whole "there's going to be this girl at the party" was just a rumor among dozens before, so who would plan?

He'd been feeling more and more guilty over the whole Angela thing anyway but now a slow tide of anger rose at having to pay for it in a way he never could have anticipated.

This the result of his first experience? Not fair, he thought, not damn fair! Bad enough having a sore dick, but this?

He paced from side to side in the kitchen, then realized he still held the phone. He placed it back in its cradle on the wall, watching the coiled wire unravel itself and snarl again like some restless snake.

Angela; Jesus. He wondered if it would be possible to track her down. Somebody ought to let her know.

Hell with that, he thought. What about Dina?

Sensations zoomed through him: relief that he hadn't had sex with Dina the past weekend, frustration for being in the situation and a sickening chill that dropped into his stomach: what to do about this?

He couldn't go to his family doctor. That guy, Dr. Kellerman, was a blabbermouth if there ever was one, always telling his parents every little thing that may have afflicted Roy. Like in high school: "Oh, he doesn't really have a flu bug, Mrs. Newsome, this is more like a cold plus a hang-over."

"Roy! You were drinking again?"

"Jeez, mom, only a little, Dr. Kellerman's just—"

"You're grounded."

Roy wanted to punch Kellerman over that one. The guy was such a jerk and Roy's mother brought out his jerkiness even more. "He complained about pain in the groin when he threw up the other day," she said on a visit when Roy was ten. And there was Kellerman with his pinky up under Roy's balls saying "turn your head and cough"—right in front of her.

No, there was no way to go to that creep.

He shambled off to sit on the front porch to think.

A swift rush of flower scent slipped into his rumination. His mother was an amazing gardener: fat red rose blooms bent the stems into arcs, a waterfall of honeysuckle hummed with bees. Dina's salt water and soap aroma teased through his mind.

He gazed around the neighborhood. Somebody was mowing their lawn up the block. A pack of little kids, round as basketballs, tumbled around the swing set across the street, screaming like banshees. Mr. Gene, across the street, was under his car in the driveway as usual, feet doing a silent dance as he worked.

Peaceful as hell, Roy thought, and I've got the clap. Shit.

A horn blast yanked him out of his thoughts. Mr. Bollins, a neighbor from up the street, had pulled up in front of the house, waving Roy to come over. As he ambled to the curb Roy realized that Bollins wanted to show off his new car. He could see the paper stuck to the side window that showed the features and price. Bollins seemed to get a new car every year, if only to parade it around. No wonder his wife had left him.

"What do ya think, Roy-o?" Bollins called, in his nicest-neighbor voice.

Roy hated being called Roy-o and Bollins well knew it. "I think it's a car, Mr. Bollins."

"Oh, hardy-har, very funny. This is the latest, Mr. Smart Guy."

"Pontiac?"

"Pontiac?! This here's a Chevy Impala, wisenheimer. Top of the line."

"Yeah, it's nice."

"Nice. Apple pie is nice; this is the car of the future, Roy-o."

Tired of playing the foil, Roy nodded and walked around the car. It was pretty nice, he had to admit. A kind of silvery blue and long as a damned battle ship. He and Dina could live in that back seat with room to spare. And Bollins certainly needed the spacious front seat with his massive gut like a mud slide against the steering wheel.

Reaching the driver side, he smiled to notice the tattoo on Bollins' ample forearm—a bare-breasted mermaid from his World War II Navy days. Roy had gone to high school with Bollins' stuck-up daughter; it always amused him to see her go red and rigid when he mentioned her father's tattoo—which he did, frequently. She was at University of Maryland now, he reflected. Maybe he should tell Phil to seduce the little princess, give her the nail.

Bollins' moon face was beaming up at him in expectation.

"Yeah, it's pretty okay, Mr. Bollins," Roy said, amused when the man's face fell.

"Well, thanks for the approval, your highness. Jesus, you kids—nothin's good enough. Anyway, tell your old man I'll be back around dinner time so he can eat his heart out."

"Sure thing. Though I think we're having spaghetti so he'll be full already."

"Hilarious, Roy-o; you're a regular comedian!"

Bollins peeled out suddenly, making Roy leap back. He could hear the guy laughing as the car zipped away.

Fat-ass, Roy thought. And then he snapped his fingers as a lightbulb went off in his head.

Ten minutes later he pulled up in front of the little bungalow that served as the office for Dr. Vokker, known around the nearby neighborhoods as "Doc Darts" for his penchant for fixing every woe with a shot of penicillin.

Blubber-butt Bollins was practically a scarecrow compared to Vokker, whose terraced beef rarely left the creaking chair in his office. Usually unshaven, his hair was always perfectly combed, the dense gleaming black of it contrasting with the gray thicket of stubble coating his wobbling chins.

When Roy was a kid, Vokker was the doctor of necessity for his family and most of the neighborhood. His office was at the intersection of several main roads where their community and others had sprung up like so many mushrooms after a rain. Vokker was in easy reach for the inevitable childhood maladies and inexpensive, a boon to the blue collar world around him.

Roy's family had moved from Baltimore city to Northshire, a new development, in 1948 and there was little nearby in the way of amenities—the nearest grocery store was a fifteen minute drive. Vokker had cornered the medical market for a time.

And no matter the malady, Vokker's menu for healing consisted primarily of two items: aspirin and penicillin. When Roy was brought in for an infection of some kind, something aspirin couldn't help, Vokker would yank open his desk drawer, whip out a ready syringe and bang!—right into the arm. Roy couldn't image how many needles were stashed in there but Vokker certainly never had to get out of his chair to get one.

When his parents finally got a second car, Vokker was dropped like a hot rivet in favor of that creep Kellerman with his shiny office in Dundalk.

Roy took a few shaky breaths, then went into the doctor's house. A scrawny woman wearing a baggy dress looked up from her magazine at him with a squint.

"Yeah?"

"I need to see Dr. Vokker."

"What's the nature of your visit?"

"Oh, uh, well, it's personal."

A tiny curlicue of a smile creased a corner of her thin lips, then vanished. Roy felt his face burning.

"Okay," she said. "Five minutes. Have a seat." She pushed a button on her phone and a faint buzz rasped from behind Vokker's door.

Roy sat as far from her as he could, pretending to be interested in an issue of Reader's Digest. It was three years old but what difference did that make? "Laughter, the Best Medicine" was always good for a little diversion.

Time ticked by; everybody has a different idea of what five minutes is, he reflected.

Finally, the woman's phone buzzed.

"Okay," she said and waved at him.

He went to the door and hesitated, wondering if he should knock.

"Just go in," rasped the woman at his back.

He pushed the door open. Behind the desk, looking even more gargantuan than Roy remembered, Vokker gazed at him, an unlit cigar plugged in the center of his mouth. Roy closed the door and walked to the chair. Vokker placed the cigar butt in an ashtray that was the shape of a human heart. He could smell the alcohol on the fat man's breath from across the room.

"So?"

"Oh, ummm, yes, doctor, I uh, well—" Roy's mouth went completely dry.

"Okay, we'll play twenty questions: Can't get it up, can't keep it down, pooping green, got a worm, athlete's foot, the clap, hair falling out, hemmo—"

"That. The cl—um, gonorrhea."

"Shocking."

"W-what?"

"A little levity, son. Anyway, too bad but it happens. You might stay away from hookers."

Roy lurched forward in the chair. "No, I—"

"Jesus, kid, calm down. I might have to tune up your funny bone, if you have one."

Roy didn't know what to say. There was something about older people— especially drunk ones, which Vokker clearly was at the moment—the stuff they thought was humorous, that left him feeling dusty.

"You pissing razor blades? Dripping?"

Roy nodded.

"King of diagnoses!" Vokker chortled, gave himself mock applause and took a little bow on the squeaking, protesting chair.

Roy tried to smile, playing along, aching for this idiocy to be finished.

"Okay, okay, floorshow's over," Vokker said, "Come over here and drop 'em."

Roy walked around the desk at the pace of a condemned man. He undid his belt, unzipped and started to push his pants down

"Turn around, for Christ's sake!" Vokker slurred, "Not shooting into your Johnson."

Roy flushed; he turned around and eased his pants and underwear down. He glanced back at Vokker who had a syringe in each hand, looking like a blimp-sized toreador.

"Bend over a bit. And relax, for God's sake. Big doses, so it goes slow."

Roy obeyed and an instant later he felt a sharp intrusion into each ass cheek. Vokker panted a little as he pushed the plungers down. The pressure was intense— it felt like fires being ignited in him.

Finally, Vokker yanked the syringes out with a flourish.

"Pull 'em up. This'll clear up in about a week. Maybe less."

Roy felt an abrupt weakness in his knees; Vokker hadn't swabbed him before or after the shot. What if he got infected from the shots on top of everything else?

"Come on, already, with the pants: your ass ain't some work of art."

Roy hastily pulled his clothes back up.

"Okay, ten bucks," Vokker said.

Roy paid him and headed out of the office as quickly as he could go. Before he could get through the front door he heard Vokker shout: “And stay away from those hookers!”

The woman at the desk released a chicken-like cackle. Roy threw open the front door and escaped into the sunlight, gasping with embarrassment.

That evening, Dina called. She was full of chit-chat about crazy things happening at her job and how the ocean was starting to sprout jellyfish, as it did every year in late July.

“Lot of surfers peeing on each other,” she giggled.

“That works?”

“Hell, no—it makes it even worse, stings about ten times more, but you can’t tell those guys anything, they’ve got salt water for brains.”

“You ever been stung?”

“Oh, yeah. Nasty experience, believe me. I’m pretty much done with the water at this point because of those damn things. Hey, when you coming down?”

“Oh, um, I—” he stammered, “I gotta check the assignments tomorrow; they keep changing stuff up. This weekend’s good, I think, but, yeah, gotta check up on the old board.”

“You didn’t already?” she asked.

He had. He was free for the weekend. He was also infected and didn’t know for how long. It was Monday; with luck he’d be okay by Saturday. With luck. And he’d use that condom from his wallet, no matter what.

“Nope; forgot.”

“Hmm, well,” she said, clearly disappointed. She shifted to a teasing tone: “Guess the honeymoon’s over. I mean, if we ever have one.”

“We will.”

“You promise?”

"You know I do. You even have to ask that?"

"Well, come on, first it's me being Harriet Hesitant and now you, Ricky Reluctant."

"You said you were okay with it," he said, too quickly.

"Whoa-whoa, I was just joking. What's going on?"

"Nothing. I just—I mean, hell, none of this is easy."

"What do you mean 'this'?" Her voice had changed.

"You know." He dropped his voice, even though his parents were in the other room, TV blasting. "Sex."

"Well, now, it's not like we don't want to, right?" she said with a lilt.

He hesitated a second too long.

"Right?" she repeated. "Is there something wrong, Roy?"

"No! Jesus! Nothing!"

"Well, do you? Want to?"

"You know I do. I have been. But, I mean, with all this holding off, it's like, I don't know, it feels kind of like a bigger deal now, like a tidal wave or something."

"It's just making love, Roy," she said, softly.

"I know, but it's gotten to be this thing, maybe just in my head, I don't know, but it's like there's all this pressure."

"You mean, what, to, um—perform?"

"Well, yeah." He gritted his teeth at the image. He couldn't picture anything like that happening to him, but who knew for sure? Everything around him seemed alien now.

I need to go to a library and do some research on this nail thing, he thought.

"Oh, Roy," she said, voice going sweet and soft. "I just want to be with you, that's all. Just us making a little old private world. No judgment on anything, okay? I never would judge you, no matter what, don't you know that?"

"I guess." He felt backed against a wall now, lying to her, making up an argument. Why shouldn't he just tell her? Why not go down the Ocean this weekend and tell her every bit of what had happened?

Because, a voice in his brain said, she'll drop you like a hot potato. You know she will.

"Hey," she said, her voice tiny, "Where'd you go?"

"Nowhere," he said. "Dina, look, I agree with everything you just said. It's all about us and nothing else. Everything is okay, no matter what happens, right? I absolutely agree."

"You sure?" she sounded like a worried child.

"Positive."

"Cross your heart?"

"Hope to die, raise my pinkie to the sky."

"Okay then," she said, feigning petulance. "I love you, doofus; I hope you know that."

"I love you, too, Mrs. Doofus."

They chatted a while longer, his apprehension slowly fading, though his stomach remained in a knot long after they hung up. He hated being like this with her. He felt as if he'd turned into the bragging jackass from the mill, telling his sex story lies. That guy doesn't deserve his wife, he thought. Am I worthy of Dina? He fervently hoped so. Who else in the world got him the way she did, who loved him without reservations?

His family certainly didn't get him, treated him like a Martian most of the time. Making up a presentable reality to appease them was the only choice he had to earn what they thought of as love. "Be a good boy" was all they said, all they seemed to care about, while he wanted to be anything but. Roy ached restlessly with a desire to be something, know something, do something—to find a place where he was whole, instead of endlessly lacking.

After they hung up he fell hollowed out, frustrated at how things were going.

His unceasing mantra: "I just want one thing to be perfect, just once, just one damned time."

What perfection was he had no clue whatsoever. Before Dina, he just knew that his lungs never felt fillable, his body seemed vacant, as if he wasn't intended to fully occupy it. At other times he felt like someone condemned to live in a glass box, watching on and never able to connect.

In high school, frustration with his family spilled into confrontations over ridiculous things at times—getting into pointless arguments with teachers or other kids. Then in an instant he be Crazy-funny Roy or Cool-cat Roy. Not many people could tolerate the swings. Phil Camber managed somehow—being an easy-going guy he tempered Roy with humor.

Johnny Monkton, on the other hand, was Roy's other best buddy precisely because he didn't put up with Roy's crap.

"Tell you what, slick," Monkton said one night when Roy was being a pain in everybody's neck. "You wanna be a fucking psycho, take it down the road, okay? Come back when you stop being a jerk-off."

Roy appreciated being talked to that honestly. He didn't know why it was a rare thing but it was.

Even his entry into the worlds of art and books and film didn't fully quell the longing in him when his anxieties came roaring through, turning him deaf and blind to anything that normally mattered. At those times, nothing was good enough, satisfying, worth the trouble.

With Dina he could breathe. And just be. He hadn't known how badly he'd wanted that, needed it, until she'd somehow slipped past his guard and made him feel like an okay guy.

But now, well, he was in a big fat web and hating it.

On the next morning's visit to the bathroom he noticed that the sensations of discomfort were a bit less. Or so he hoped.

He didn't work until the afternoon—3-11 shift. It was his favorite in many ways since hanging out reading late at night then sleeping in the next day was his preferred rhythm.

The house was silent, as usual on a weekday, with both parents off to their jobs. He made some toast, reheated the coffee his mother left for him and settled in over The Dharma Bums, his second venture into Kerouac. It was so different from On the Road—that book made him hold his breath with anticipation and triggered an incessant rise of wildness in his blood to the point where he was ready to steal a car himself and tear through the American underbelly. The Dharma Bums was more reflective; it made him appreciate the part of himself that enjoyed solitude.

After a few chapters, he began to feel restless. He went out to his car and just started driving. It was that same old sensation: the need to be moving, to be anywhere different, no matter where the current "here" was—just elsewhere.

It was a beautiful day; hot without being oppressive. He thought of driving out to the shore parks along the rivers but there would probably be people he knew and he wasn't up for it. For a while he let the car decide, taking any right turn that came up, then any left.

Eventually he found himself on Eastern Boulevard, heading into Essex. He decided to go to the community college, just to look around.

He had no idea what was propelling him, though he smiled to think he might run into somebody there who had heard of Kerouac. Fat chance of that at work; most of those guys thought reading books was for fags—their word—and limp dick sissies. He had tried to have a conversation about writers with one guy, telling him about Henry Miller's book Nexus, but giving up when the guy interrupted with: "Well, I mean, are there any guns or, like, cool cars in this here book of yours?"

Dina hadn't read as much as Roy, of course, being more visually oriented, but she loved hearing him talk about books. She always asked him to give her what he'd finished and would come back with tons of comments that showed him new things about the book. In exchange she brought him some books on artists she loved, teaching him a language beyond words.

Roy pulled into the white rock parking lot of the community college and gazed around. The "campus" was temporary, with new land purchased on some rolling hills about twenty miles away, waiting for somebody to push the "go" button to start construction. There were two brown wood-shingled buildings, musty with creaky wooden floors, that served as offices and classrooms,. Around the buildings a scattering of trailers served as additional classrooms plus two designated just for student use: the "recreation" trailer and the "study" trailer. The rec trailer was where most of the kids hung out, practicing rowdiness and clumsy seduction.

The study trailer, on the other hand, was the secret lair of the people Roy most related to: the misfit big brains who put their energies into plotting creative revenge on certain professors or crafting crazy schemes to steal things from the rec trailer.

They were always coming up with lunatic ideas: hosting faux events like "Kick a Puppy Day" and breaking into spirited hootenannies when anyone with a guitar showed up. His love of folk music was nurtured there by people bringing in records by Dave Van Ronk and Big Bill Broonzy. And Dylan, of course, mixed in with The Beatles, Simon and Garfunkel, Joan Baez.

Roy walked around, peering through trailer windows. The school only had one summer session, in June, so much of the place was locked up. He went into the building where the English faculty had offices, wondering if anybody was around. He half-hoped to run into Mr. Verdeen, one of his favorite professors. Verdeen had won Roy's heart in class one day when a perpetually clueless kid named Olivetti interrupted the lecture to ask, "Mr. Verdeen, I don't understand what you said about this guy Lord Byron. What's 'dark and brooding,'?"

Verdeen paused for the briefest of seconds and said, "Well, Mr. Olivetti, it's the opposite of blond and doltish, such as yourself."

Roy almost felt bad for the kid as a wash of laughter swamped the room.

The offices were locked. Roy continued to wander. He stopped at the end of the hallway to look at a bulletin board covered in layers with flyers and handwritten notes, many spilling over the side or taped to the wall. There were notices for concerts and "Ban the Bomb" events, used textbooks for sale, campus movie nights, lists of courses being offered for the fall semester, invitations to join various clubs and a few handwritten notes: "Ken, call Barbie—the rabbit died,""Found, one pair tortoise shell sunglasses," and "LBJ, go home: we cancelled your war."

He tried the handle of a classroom and found it unlocked. Stepping inside, he was thrust back in time. He took the seat where he normally sat for the Intro to Theatre Class with Mr. Lyter. He smiled to remember how Lyter always bounced the chalk in his palm as he paced up and down in front of the room, talking in endless circles. The students made bets as to how long it would be before absent-minded Lyter dropped the chalk, which he always did.

He closed his eyes, picturing the people in the class. The intoxicating scent of Alice Carmody's perfume and the out-thrust of her ample chest came to his senses somehow accompanied by the memory of Dr. Andrews down the hall, lecturing on Political Science in his carnival barker voice. The chair Roy was sitting in might have been new in the 1950s, but now its wooden desk surface was dull, initials scratched into it and strangely warm to the touch.

Roy smiled as he trailed his palm along the wood.

He eased back, resting his head, letting his thoughts do laps. He'd been a shitty student, he knew, too caught up in the social aspect of college and his fascination with the art and literary worlds he'd stumbled onto in the city.

It was when he started college that "being elsewhere" became his mission; the discovery that people—that he—could leave campus or just not show up for class was irresistible after twelve years of public school imprisonment. His joke was that his major was cutting class, but it was true.

Images from the study trailer drifted in: the day everyone talked only in fake Russian; a late afternoon, bitter winter outside while inside everyone huddled around a Sterno can, making S'mores; the many times he sat on a couch and let the voices around him weave in and out—George with his easy joking and Richard's slightly affectatious chatter; the sound of Barb and Julie harmonizing through their luminously slowed version of the Beatles' "Please Please Me."

Roy sat up abruptly in the silent classroom. In a white heat he saw that something important had slipped through his hands. It wasn't enough for him to seek out movies and books on his own. It was the give and take with other people that made school way more than just sitting in a classroom. There was something in that, some energy or lifeblood. "Please Please Me" on a December afternoon kiting upward on sweet female voices with the scent of coming snow ghosting the air.

He wasn't destined for life in the reek and crush of the steel mill. No, that was nothing but brutally hard surfaces, impervious to human touch and indifferent to the simple, truthful stuff of art. What Mr. Verdeen called "the life of the mind"—that's what really mattered.

"Yes!" he said into the still air.

He stood up, knocking over the desk chair with a percussive crash. Righting it, he raced out of the classroom and went to the pay phone at the end of the hall. He called in sick to work, let the ragging from Ed Eakins, his boss, loosen his earwax for a minute, then hung up before the guy finished.

He dashed out to his car and tore off toward Ocean City. And Dina.

Traffic on a Tuesday going down the Ocean wasn't bad at all, he realized, compared to the weekend. After a quick side-trip, he got to Mel's Shell Shack in plenty of time to surprise Dina in the store.

"What are you doing here?" she blurted, face flushing bright red around her smile.

"Well, surprise early visit, obviously," he said, "but even bigger is this," and he waved a wad of papers and a brochure at her.

"What's all th—" she started, then fixed him with wide eyes. "Salisbury? You're going to go to my school?"

"Well, apply to your school. Don't know how many people they take in with a, like, point zero five grade point average, but I'm going to give it a shot."

"Roy!" She jumped up, wrapping her legs around his waist, setting a table covered with expensive shells to jangling. Two old women watched them grayly over their bifocals. "You are amazing. I thought you were completely done with school?"

"I thought so, too," he said and recounted his morning at the community college.

"Holy god," she said, pulling him by the hand to the little back room where Mel usually hid out, sipping on a bottle. She pulled him into a kiss that left both of them panting.

Hours later, after a celebratory dinner, Roy and Dina were lounging on a couch. This apartment was another new one to Roy; it belonged to a girl named Laurel that Dina knew from an artists' studio in Salisbury. This place was a step up from the usual: modern, clean and unadorned by the typical surfer detritus.

Roy was smiling and softly riffing the lyric from "Witch Doctor," a novelty song from the Fifties.

"We are being stupid-assed," he said, with a fat grin.

"God, I know it. We're acting just like the couples we always make fun of."

"Nah, we are too cool."

"Nope; couple of real jerk-waters."

"Oh, lovey-dovey-boo-boo-baby-bearkins," he drooled, "let me take you home to mother."

"Sweetie-chickie-sugar-cheeks," she falsettoed, "Yes, oh, yes, take me to your mama-mama, do! She will love me!"

"Of course she will!"

"Or else," Dina shouted.

They laughed at themselves, then let the silliness die a natural death. A radio was on in another apartment. Dusty Springfield singing "Wishin' and Hopin.'"

The slow beat of the song lulled Roy to sleep.

He woke up abruptly, disoriented. It took a few moments to realize that Dina was straddling him, wearing only her panties.

He sat up so fast she was thrown to the side with a shriek.

"Owww!" she yelped.

His eyes were taking her body in, the whiteness of her breasts contrasting with her tan made his brain leap bright red.

"Oh, my god, Dina," he said, drawing back.

"What?" she blurted. "Don't you want me?"

"Are you kidding me? So much, Jesus Christ, I can't even begin to describe—I mean, holy god."

He grasped her hands, then fumbled for his wallet, for the condom, but his mind had begun shouting, "Don't let her touch it, put her mouth on your contagious prick, don't infect her with Angela's sickness—"

And then he was crying, everything crashing down on him at once. Face running like a bursting dam, he stumbled out of the room and into the bathroom, thrusting the door behind him.

Dina was right on his heels and caught the door with her hands, following him in. He wheeled around to see her in the doorway. She grabbed a towel and covered herself, standing rigidly still, her face a wall of confusion.

After a moment, she spoke, so softly he wasn't sure he heard anything. "What is it, Roy? You know you can talk to me."

He looked at her, his eyes blurring.

Lowering himself to sit on the edge of the bathtub, he tried to find the will to speak, to say what he had to if things would ever be right again.

Minutes passed by. Now the next door radio was playing a Peter and Gordon tune: "A World Without Love."

Dina wrapped the towel around her more securely and sat on the toilet lid, taking his hand. "Baby, please, come on. No matter what it is, it will be okay."

"You sure? You won't be mad?"

"I just want to help."

Roy looked at her, studying her face for a long while. He blew his nose, wiped his eyes, took a deep breath and plunged.

"See, there was this party and my buddy Phil Camber was back home on a break from U of M summer school," he began and started talking in such a rushing outpour of words he could barely grab a breath to stay on top of it.

He talked without punctuation while Dina watched and listened, her face steadily growing more pale and opaque as he went on, as he tried to touch on just the bare minimum of details, wanting to make it clear how disgusted he was with himself, how he'd really beaten himself up over the whole thing.

When he got to Phil's phone call and the nail, Dina leapt to her feet and went out of the room, slamming the door violently.

He hesitated then got up to follow but the door banged open again and she charged into the bathroom, now dressed.

"You bastard," she said. "You absolute fucking bastard."

Roy winced at the brutal thrust of her words.

"Are you listening?" she asked.

He nodded.

“Good. I can’t believe after everything I told you about me —about how I haven’t trusted guys for all this time and why. I cannot fucking believe you’d do this.”

“I’m sorry. Dina, I know I really messed up.”

“Oh, that you did, buddy, that you did.”

“But I got some shots and I’ll be healed up and then—” The look on her face stopped him cold.

“Jesus Christ, I’m an idiot!” She shouted to the ceiling. “I should’ve known who you really are, ‘Mr. I’m a Surfer,’ what a fucking joke. ‘Mr. I’m Not Ready.’ That just a few days ago, Roy, when you could’ve told me about the party, but oh, no, you didn’t trust me enough for that.”

“I thought you’d hate me.”

“Oh, yes, believe me, I would’ve but if you’d come straight to me and been honest at least I’d have known you respected me enough to be truthful about it.”

“I didn’t—”

“Stop.”

“Dina, I’m sorry, I’ll do anything to—“

“Stop! Look, whatever else it is you’re going to say, I’m not going to hear, okay? One of us is leavin’ in a minute and it ain’t going to be me, so get that clear in your head.”

He opened his mouth, then closed it again.

“Exactly,” she said. “Ain’t a thing you can possibly say right now. So, yeah, in a minute, you’re going, but I gotta say this: see, you come here with this business about applying to Salisbury and let me get all happy, and you’re thinking, maybe, just maybe, you’d get away with this other. Like, ‘Oh, heyyy, I’ll be all healed up and then finally we’ll do it and I’ll get away with it.’ You shit-head, you fucking rotten lying jerk. No better than any other low-life guy.”

“Dina—”

“Nope. Nope. Just get up from there and go out that door and don’t look back.”

“Come on, please, don’t let’s quit now.”

“Get out of here!”

“But—you love me, you said you loved me!”

She fixed him with a glare that stopped him cold. When she spoke, her voice was low, shaky, barely in control of herself.

“I loved who I thought you were. My mistake. You’re lucky I don’t call my cousins and have them come stomp your ass. Go.”

“Please,” he said and dropped to his knees. “Please, please forgive me.”

“No, Roy. Don’t you get it? How could I trust you again? Ever?”

“You can, I swear it!”

“Of all the things I told you about me, the one you don’t get is that when I’m done with something, I’m just flat done.”

“Dina,” he started, then shut down. What could he say now?

She turned from him, walked to the front door and thrust it open, her face closed as a fist.

He stood, wavering, feeling like some statue about to crash to the ground into a thousand pieces, wanting to say something, anything, to turn this around, to not have everything completely wiped out, but one glance at her told him it was hopeless.

She didn’t even look like Dina now but like some iron replica of her—implacable, impenetrable, emptied.

He willed himself to move, to walk to the door. He heard a shaky intake of breath as he passed her, prelude to tears he knew she wouldn’t let him see. He hesitated for a moment, then felt the dark distance that was rapidly filling the room.

He left. The door slammed behind him. A sobbing wail came from inside.

In the car he was crying again, indifferent to curious glances from passersby, his mind reeling. He started the engine and headed out toward the beach where they’d met, not thinking, rolling on instinct. When he finally focused and realized where he was he immediately made a u-turn, cutting off cars from both directions to clamorous reactions.

"Asshole!"

"Yeah, I am!" Roy shouted back. "You wanna make something of it?"

"Fuck you!" the driver bellowed.

Roy pulled to the side of the road, shaking. He couldn't think, couldn't move. Minutes drifted past like an incoming fog.

There was nothing for it. What else could he do? He headed back toward Baltimore.

Ocean City was done for him now; dead. No, he thought, I'm dead for it. Nothing but stupid endings.

He was tempted for a moment to stop off at the pool hall where he'd beaten the kid out of his cue stick, maybe get into a game, pick a fight, get the shit kicked out of him—what he deserved.

But he pressed on, heading west into the steady end of daylight, eyes tearing now from the glare of the sun.

He turned the radio on. Then off. On. Off.

Reaching into the passenger seat he grabbed the papers from the college and flung them out the window. Fuck it, he thought, fuck everything to hell.

Out on the highway, flashing past the fields of growing crops, their odors intense and heady, he pushed down on the accelerator. He watched the speedometer as the car climbed past seventy, then eighty and on to a hundred. He wanted to drive into the sky, leave the shit-heap of his life behind, drive into the sky or maybe just into a tree, end the whole circus right then and there. He kept his pedal down as the car shot through the twilight air.

At a hundred and ten the car began loping, flying over low patches and onto the higher stretches. And then it felt as if it wasn't touching the surface at all, as if he really was going to leave the burdens of gravity and thought and consequence. He had climbed onto the back of a beast that was determined to blaze into bits, filling the sky with rage and fire.

He passed over a rise in the road and the car leapt into the air with such a lift he thought it wouldn't come down. He felt weightless, exultant, then genuinely terrified.

He jerked his foot off the gas pedal. The car landed with a hard thump and a series of rattling jolts, then quickly slowed. He let out his breath.

An hour later he pulled into a gas station and filled the tank, watching moths battering themselves against the lights.

His mind continually whirled through the scene at the apartment. It was as if the ground had opened up and swallowed his entire life in one gulp.

What to do? Where to go? How to even think about anything?

Roy got back into the car and started driving.

But not to Baltimore, no.

Elsewhere, he thought. Yep: elsewhere

Like there was anywhere else, ever.

7

FEVER

Roy woke up with a banging in his head.

It took a few seconds to realize the sound was coming from outside. Somebody hammering.

He was in his car, he knew that much, conked out on the front seat. He sat up carefully, realizing as he did that he was clutching an empty pint of whiskey. Once fully upright, the battering sound throbbed between his ears.

He looked around, slowly taking in an alien landscape full of dark shapes. Huge things in piles, metal and rust, the rancid odor of grease or oil or something. Then it clicked. A junkyard. He was parked in a junkyard.

Well, not in it exactly, but pulled up at the front gate of it, just off some blank, houseless road.

Things were coming into focus. The banging sounds were being made by a guy about fifty feet away, bashing away at the side of a car.

"Mother fucking son of a bitch!" the man yelled, throwing down the hammer.

Roy was about to start up the car but a shadow to his left suddenly sharpened into the massive head of a black dog sitting a foot from his door, tall enough—even sitting—to look right into the car. The dog was panting, its dripping tongue hanging out, gazing intently at Roy. He thought better of moving. The hammer guy was walking back and forth, wiping his hands on a rag already black with grease, still cursing.

Roy tried to figure out how he'd gotten there. He'd been drinking, so okay, where did he get the bottle? He remembered pushing the car to the highest speed he dared, then getting spooked by it. Then stopping at a gas station and leaving the place and driving aimlessly for a bit and then? Oh, right, he'd gone into Salisbury and gotten some old guy to buy the whiskey for him. Okay, but still, how had he ended up here at the front gate of this car graveyard?

No answers were forthcoming.

The dog made a sound like a yawn, panted harder for a moment, then snapped his jaws shut and dropped out of view, appearing again in a shady spot a few yards away.

Roy started the car. He wanted to back up but there was another dog, dark brown and equally enormous, sitting behind him on the road.

He felt trapped. His stomach gurgled in a way that made him swallow hard half a dozen times. When he looked down from the rear view mirror, Roy saw that the man was now standing in front of the car.

"Hey," the man said, still wiping his hands on the rag.

Roy leaned out of the window, pushing the door lock down with his arm as he did.

"Morning," he said.

"Morning?" the man barked a laugh. "Past noon, buddy. Ought to charge you for parking in my driveway."

"Yeah. Sorry. I didn't mean to. I was—" Roy stopped short of saying he was drunk. "I was too sleepy to keep driving, so I pulled over where I could."

"More like too blotto. Can smell you from here. Ought to charge you," the guy said again and leaned over to dribble a long brown stream of spit on the ground, wiping his mouth on his shirt sleeve. "I let you sleep it off. But I gotta wrecker comin' by any minute, won't be able to get past you."

"Okay," Roy said, trying to be affable, "I can move. I need to go anyway."

"Crusher, come here," the man called. Roy watched while the massive brown dog trotted from behind his car to the man. "What do you think we ought to charge this kid for parking here illegal and all? Huh? Or maybe call the law 'cause of him bein' drunk?"

Roy put on a big smile to show he was in on the joke while he inched the gear shift out of Park into Reverse. He eased the car back a foot.

"Where the fuck do you think you're goin'? Parkin' ain't free! I ain't jokin' around with you, boy!"

Roy didn't answer. He ducked his head back in, floored the gas pedal and rocketed out onto the road, He threw the lever into Drive and nearly spun out trying to get purchase on the gravel.

"Git!" the man yelled. It took a few seconds to realize the guy wasn't talking to him but the dogs, who morphed into black and brown streaks racing toward the car.

The car wheels found the roadway and he shot forward, the dogs in barking pursuit. Something clanged off the trunk but Roy didn't look back or lift his foot from the pedal.

He turned a corner feeling the car lean dangerously and kept going, the dogs receding in his mirror.

He couldn't risk slowing down. What if those dogs knew some shortcut through the brush and woods he was flitting past? A vision of open jaws preceding the leap of a monstrous canine body through his car window made him shudder.

His window was already up by now; he leaned precariously to wind up the passenger side glass.

A stop sign in the distance was daring him to keep going. He wanted to run it but what was past it? His luck today, some motorcycle cop would be just licking his chops for an easy catch.

He eased back on the gas, feeling the car shaking beneath him as it settled out of high speed, the tires juddering over every ragged flaw in the roadway.

He pulled up to the red, bullet-pocked octagon and looked around.

Where the hell am I?

All he could see to his left was an ocean of corn stalks. On the right, a drainage ditch, scrub and some trailer homes. Black jockey figures, pink flamingos and bird baths abounded.

After debating for a moment, he followed his instinct and turned right. It took a few more guesses until he finally emerged onto Route 50. To his left was the business district of Salisbury. He turned in that direction, wanting a bathroom and hoping for some place to buy some aspirin.

The air was filled with fumes that didn't help his hang-over: diesel fuel, cooking odors that felt like gobs of grease being spooned into his nose, the blunt rise of heat from the roadway, his own body funk.

Not much chance, he thought, of not barfing in the near future. He swallowed and swallowed against the fetid acid rising in his throat. He pulled into the lot of a place that sold cigarettes, milk and a small assortment of groceries. He bought a container of orange juice, some chewable baby aspirin and used the reeking, filthy bathroom, retching into the sink until he was dizzy.

Once he was back on the main drag, he remembered the turns to where Dina lived. It took a lot to just keep going straight.

An hour later, he was nearing the ocean. He still felt like a punching bag from the aftermath of getting drunk and sleeping with his head tilted against the arm rest. His stomach was a bit less queasy. The tide of orange juice rolling around in it hadn't been the smartest choice but he couldn't face food yet.

He felt feverish from inside but his forehead was cool, clammy. He changed his shirt in the car but felt no fresher.

It was mid-afternoon. He didn't know what to do with himself, other than drive down the Ocean. It was a dead place for him now but he couldn't think of anywhere else to go.

Going home would be a really bad idea since he'd called in sick the day before and there was no way his dad wouldn't know about it. He dreaded the encounter. His father didn't yell at him and was never a hitter, so Roy escaped some of the fates his friends had suffered. Then again, they hadn't experienced The Talk.

No matter the subject, no matter how egregious Roy's given screw-up, the resultant aftermath was being sat down for The Talk. His father would quietly delineate Roy's current misdemeanor, review previous offenses, remind Roy that he came from a good home, and that his mother loved him (never mentioning his own feelings about Roy—if he had any), and then settle in for at least an hour of life lessons from what Roy thought of as "Dad's Big Book of Cautionary Tales."

Roy always tried hard to listen. In some ways he really liked hearing his dad's stories of growing up in the Depression era in Baltimore City. The many times his family had been dislocated, going steadily down in neighborhood quality after his own father had died, being evicted, their furniture tossed in the street. The ability to survive all that and become a high level general foreman at Bethlehem Steel was Horatio Alger stuff.

His mother's struggle was also tough. She grew up in the North Carolina backwoods where her father was, as she put it, "a night rider," meaning the Klan, and where she was fobbed off from sister to aunt to cousin for living accommodations. She'd been determined to finish high school and did, then when World War II started emigrated north to find work and a new life. She just didn't seem to cling to her past the way his dad did or feel the need to trot it out over and over.

Roy respected the way both his parents had overcome really difficult childhoods and made something of themselves. Hell, they'd met working as ship fitters for Bethlehem Steel during the war—he a day laborer and she a welder. They were All-American successes.

Even so, having the Dad stories repeated over and over until he could parrot them practically verbatim was like someone scratching their initials deep into his forehead with a ragged fingernail. Whenever his dad sat Roy down, his mother would make herself scarce, retreating into the kitchen. Roy knew she saw how it would wear him down, deflate him. He also knew she'd be making something special for him in the place where she held domain.

"Here," she'd say as he dragged into the room, and hold out a small plate with something chocolate on it. "It's a recipe I found for you to try out for me, see if you like it. Your father can try his for dessert after dinner."

Roy would sit in the kitchen, slowly picking through the treat and trying to enjoy it, though it was a struggle—he always felt so worthless after any of The Talks.

So: no. The Talk could wait. Especially at this moment when he was so angry he might tell his father to shove his old stories. Not, he knew, the most prudent choice.

There was really nowhere else to go. He had no one to call, no friends to visit. He could drive into Baltimore city, maybe spend the day taking shit from Abe Sherman in the book store or drinking in a corner at Martick's, where carding kids was considered uncool—as long as the kid was cool. But then what?

So, yes, okay, down the Ocean, dead to him or not. Stay in town, on the boardwalk or the amusement centers, sleep in the car again but far from his normal spot out by the dunes. He'd never go to that part of the beach again.

Dina.

God damn it. No, he thought in the next instant: not it: me.

He wanted to see her. He doubted he would. Most likely she was somewhere back in Salisbury with her family or holed up at one of her friends' apartments. He might have passed her on the street last night as he drove around, the booze squishing his brain to a soggy pancake.

He couldn't release the claw that had reached down his throat and seized his guts. Just getting a full breath took a conscious effort. His chest felt like someone was standing on it.

He had always assumed that heartache was just a metaphor, an image; not so.

Every young woman he saw reminded him of her, no matter how different they were in appearance, because they weren't her.

He needed to see her. He couldn't stand the memory of how she looked at him before he left. The way she stared as if he was nothing more than a worm. It's what he saw now in the mirror.

He berated himself, gave the thoughts voice and pounded angrily on the steering wheel, turned the radio up as loud as it could go hoping to burst his eardrums, punched his face a dozen times and ended up pulled on to the shoulder, gripping the steering wheel with all his might, hoping to break it or shatter his hands, wanting nothing more than to turn to dust.

Why, he thought, why do I always screw up? Della, Dina, a raft of other relationships floated by—all bad choices, over and over, every relationship a failure.

He wanted to blame Phil. Blame Angela, but what difference would that make? Nobody told me to stick my dick in her, I just had a chance and took it and that's all my fault, nobody else's. Could've said "no" to the party, could've stayed away from the Arundel corner altogether—it's where too many crazy nights got started—but not Roy, not pathetic dumb-ass Roy.

He pulled back on the road, finally, knowing that the only thing that could help was to stay in motion. It was slow going. He had to pull over a number of times to throw up on the roadside. His insides felt orange from the juice and the aspirins.

When he arrived in Ocean City in the late afternoon he was astonished to find a parking spot within minutes, then remembered it was a Wednesday—transition day for people leaving and arriving. He went to the boardwalk and began moving restlessly along with the shambling crowds. He was ravenous instantly from the assault of smells: caramel popcorn, cotton candy, hot dogs. A pizza place flirted briefly but the only thing he knew he could hold down was the fries at Thrasher's.

Walking along with a small cup of the greasy potatoes, letting the heat at the bottom of it burn his hand, Roy only saw ugliness all around. Families trudged along in sun-bit disarray, the kids picking at each other, getting underfoot, catching the occasional smack from the farmer-tanned dad. Teenagers were slouching around, posing their sexuality or jittering about like mental patients. A whole world was heaving past: fat women, fatter men, sunburned people of all descriptions. The reek in the air of cooking oil, the coconut cloy of sun tan lotion choked him. Everything made his brain reel and his stomach threaten to revolt. He ate as slowly as he could.

He stood at the railing staring at the beach, as if answers would materialize. All he saw was sand littered with prostrate bodies, looking like the aftermath of a massive battle. The ocean rose and fell and retreated.

What difference did any of it make, he thought. None of this is mine. I might as well be from outer space.

He stayed there a long while, eating as slowly as he could manage. The salt and apple cider vinegar seemed to ease his gut somewhat.

He thought about the guy at the junk yard for a minute, yo-yoing between wanting to go back there and run the jerk over or apologize. He'd never blacked out from drinking before. How he'd ended up there was a complete mystery. He pictured another ending to the previous night: dying in a burning car on the side of some highway. He shook the image away.

By the time he reached the bottom of the container, the day's temperature was starting to drop a bit. The sun was behind him now, casting long shadows across the beach. Bronze-orange guys and girls with white zinc oxide on their noses were whistling up and down, signaling with red flags and easing down from their lifeguard stands. Others were retrieving rental umbrellas and folding chairs. Solitary men flying kites seemed to have sprouted from the sand. The air's tang of leaf rot was letting everybody know that the end of summer was only a series of sunsets away.

Roy sighed. The end of a beach day was always melancholy and even more so now. Nothing looked more desolate than the expanse of empty sand. There were always the last stragglers hanging on to the day and posses of kids still trying to build the Best Sand Castle Ever but they were merely random dots on the long tongue of graying shoreline. Hermit monks with metal detectors were slowly sweeping segments of the beach, praying for treasure.

The neon lights of the boardwalk were coming on bit by bit, pale against the fading daylight. Seagulls were scavenging. Girls going by now smelled of soap and shampoo instead of sun tan lotion.

The restless crash of the ocean on the emptying beach felt like some commentary on the way things came and went, all the time. He imagined the thousands of shipwrecks, the millions of drowned bodies populating the depths and the uncountable numbers of sea things swimming about.

"I am one depressing guy," he said with a sharp laugh to some gulls that were edging from side to side on the railing. Several were white and gray, but one had a black head and tail feathers that grabbed his attention until he remembered that Dina had showed him some sketches of that kind of gull.

Annoyed, he tossed the last bits of potatoes at the stupid birds and chucked the empty container toward a trash can, missing the first time, picking up the bucket and slamming it in angrily.

A few blocks down, music caught his ear—"Dancing in the Street." There was a hotel with a big veranda on the second floor. Some kids, most of them looking to be around his age, were dancing and whooping it up.

Oh yay, goodie, he thought morosely, a party. Whoopee.

He started walking again.

"Roy!"

He kept moving. Nobody could be calling his name.

"Ro-o-o-o-y-e-e-e!" came the voice again, rising to a shriek.

He turned to look. Leaning on the balcony railing and waving wildly was a girl he knew from high school. What was it? Karen? Nope, no, ah: Kimberly. Kimberly Ebersol. She'd been in the Social Studies class with him and Camber. He couldn't think of anything else he knew about her—just another girl.

He waved a half-gesture back and turned down the boardwalk again.

When he heard the sound of someone walking rapidly up behind him, he groaned inwardly. Oh, sure, hi, how are ya, no I don't want to come to your dumb party, any party, nice seein' ya, bye.

"You look like shit," came the voice behind him.

What the hell could he say to that? He turned to see her standing there with a wide grin.

"Hi to you, too."

"Seriously, Roy, you look like your whole family just died."

"That's because they did, Kimberly."

Her face morphed into a tragic mask for a moment before the lightbulb went off.

"Oh, you," she said, "always the big joker."

"Yeah, me," he said through a brittle grin.

"So for real, how've you been? I haven't seen you since graduation. I couldn't believe it was you I was seeing. I was like, 'Is that good old Newson? Guess I oughta find out or not' and well, hey—" She stopped talking and gazed at him with a hopeful smile.

“I’m okay,” he said, making the best effort he could manage.

“Well, good. I didn’t mean to sound like I was criticizing you or nothin’. You just looked down in the dumps.”

“Down in the junk yard, more like,” he said with a short laugh.

“Huh?”

When he didn’t explain she went on: “You should come up to the party. It’s this guy’s birthday or something—he’s rented out the whole upstairs front part of the hotel. I don’t know him but me and Nancy, we wanted to see inside that place. It’s pretty cool. He was talking to us on the beach, so—” She shrugged and left her thoughts hanging again.

He smiled to recall that about her from class—she never seemed to get to whatever point she was trying to make.

He also remembered other things now that they were standing there. She was wearing some kind of gauzy see-through jacket over a modest black and white plaid two-piece bathing suit or two-piece something or other. He couldn’t be bothered with all the names girls had for the clothes they wore. The jacket hid her body except for her flat stomach and long legs.

What surged in from his memory was her hourglass shape. She didn’t display it like some of the girls at school but you couldn’t miss that body, no matter what she was wearing. He wondered if she’d ever been with Phil. He remembered checking her out in the classroom on a regular basis, speculating.

He realized she was watching him look her over now. Roy glanced away, putting on a frozen smile.

“Don’t you want to come to the party? These guys, they made this, I don’t know, spiked punch and it’s really...” She searched for the right word then said: “Really wow-ee, ya know?”

"Tell you the truth Kimberly, I'm so far from wow-ee right now I'm on another planet."

"Mars," she said, giggling, her face flushed and feverish. There was a thin glaze of sweat on her forehead.

"More like Pluto," he said, trying not to snap at her.

"Mickey's dog!" she chirped and did a Mickey Mouse falsetto: "Here Pluto, here boy!"

Roy's smile was a rictus now, rigid face holding back his desire to scream at this stupid girl.

"Ha, yeah," he said. "Really good Mickey, yep. Okay, so you take care, Kimberly."

Roy turned and started away. He came to a halt after three steps as she grabbed the tail of his shirt. He wheeled about, ready to tell her off in clear terms. She was looking agitated now.

"Oh, come on, please? Just come to the party for a bit. Nancy wants to stay and those guys are getting pretty smashed and so is she. I'm getting kinda nervous. And anyway, I've told her all about you and Phil Camber in that boring Social Studies class, how you guys were always joking around and making us laugh and pissing off old Mrs. Pickle-Head."

She looked like a helpless little kid. His anger flushed away.

"Yeah, okay. Just for a bit."

"Oh, good. Maybe you can talk Nancy into leaving. We'll all go someplace, maybe."

"We'll see," he said.

Upstairs, the music was playing on. Kimberly pulled him by the hand up the steps and toward a short, stocky girl who was clearly drunk, dancing by herself, her hair sweated to her forehead. What was that joke? "Girls don't sweat—they have glow." Nancy's glow was dripping down her face in rivulets.

"Nance, this is Roy. I told you all about him," Kimberly said, finger-combing the tangles from the girl's face, her nails long and bright red.

"Hey, Roy, you old buddy of Kimmy-Kim's, how you doin'?"

"Oh, just peachy-dandy, Nancy."

""Peachy-dandy,'" she repeated with a guffaw. "You were right, Kim-o, this guy is a funny old shit!"

"Nancy!" Kimberly hissed in mock disapproval. "Let me get you some punch, Roy," she said with a flounce and pivoted away.

"Um, oh, no," Roy began, but she was already at the bowl.

Nancy was looking him up and down, her face corkscrewed into a ruddy smirk.

"Some kinda-kinda party, right Ray?"

"Roy."

"Yeah, that."

"Sure, it's some kinda party, Francie."

"Ha, I get what you did there. You're one funny shit."

"Funniest. Shittiest. Got it all covered."

Nancy guffawed loudly. Several people turned around.

Kimberly returned, juggling three cups of punch, sloshing liquid as she went.

"Well, Roy, here's to the great class of '63 and seeing you again!"

"Boola-boola," Roy said.

"Fuckin'-A," said Nancy with a burp.

He realized he didn't feel shocked now at that word coming out of a girl's mouth. Roll with the times, man. "Fucking A through Z," he said.

The girls cheered and they all clinked. Nancy tossed hers down while Kimberly and Roy took more modest sips.

The punch was some concoction of pineapple juice and some other fruit juice he couldn't distinguish, and a ton of booze. No wonder Nancy was so far gone, throwing them back like that.

He stood with the girls, watching the party surge and wane with each new record dropping onto the turntable. Some people were dancing, a couple intertwined on a rattan chair were making out, guys were catcalling down at girls passing by on the boardwalk.

Kimberly made another run to the punch bowl, leaving Nancy's cup there. Roy gulped his this time, feeling the alcohol paw at the edges of his hangover.

He was ready to split now. He turned toward Kimberly, apology ready at his lips, only to see Nancy start to wobble off into the hotel room. She took a few steps, made a valiant effort to reach the bed but collapsed on the floor instead, pulling the bed covers down, breaking her fall.

"Oh, crap on a cracker," Kimberly said, rushing into the room. Roy was right behind her. They helped Nancy up on the bed, her head lolling around loosely.

"Oh, man," Kimberly said. "This again."

"Again?"

"Yeah, I knew I shoulda been countin' her drinks. Now we're stuck here until I can get her vertical. I mean..."

"That's a drag."

"Yeah, no kidding." She looked at Roy, biting her lower lip worriedly. "Do you mind? Staying for a bit? Like I said, I don't know these guys."

"They look okay to me."

"Roy. Stuff can happen to passed out girls—really bad stuff; you know what I'm sayin'..."

"Yeah, but—"

"It won't be long. Please? Maybe an hour and then I'll get her up, I promise."

He glanced at Nancy. She was lying face down, her legs apart. He could see red panties or a bathing suit bottom peeking out from inside one leg of her disarrayed shorts.

"Um," he said, nodding at the sight then quickly looking away. Images of Angela's naked body and Dina in her panties swirled through his head.

Kimberly adjusted Nancy's position, smoothing the girl's clothes down, then sat on the edge of the bed pushing the hair from Nancy's damp forehead again.

"Okay, an hour," he said, walking around to the other side of the bed and sitting. Like I have somewhere to be, he thought.

"Here," Kimberly said, "might as well have another drink while we wait, right?"

She was gone before he could say anything and returned juggling several larger cups. He watched the way her body moved, then glanced away.

They clinked and drank. Roy tossed his down, hoping to chase the hang-over completely away. Kimberly sipped, watching him over the rim of her cup.

The room was cool, a bit musty. With no lights on, the view through the door was like watching a vertical movie. Bodies moved by, dancing, clowning; the music kept flowing through. "A Summer Song" by two British guys, Chad and Jeremy, was on now. Hadn't he heard that with Dina that time when—

He shoved the thought away.

"I need to lean back," Kimberly announced as she moved around to his side of the bed, slipping off her sandals and the gauzy jacket. He moved so she could sit against the headboard and stretch her legs out in front of her.

"My back still gives me trouble," she said. He looked blank. "I was in that car wreck with Jimmy Krionitis?"

"Oh, yeah, that's right."

"If I stand too long or sit without support, it starts to ache on me. It don't help to be heavy on top, neither," she said with a throw-away chuckle.

He nodded, not knowing what to say to that. He shifted toward the bottom of the bed to make more room for her legs.

"You don't have to move."

"I don't mind."

“Well, you can turn toward me, anyway,” she teased.

She plucked at his shirt with her toes. He eased around to face her. He could feel the alcohol softly singing in his brain.

“There you are,” she said. “God, I remember you and Camber so well. Funny guys. Cute, too.”

“Well, Phil, for sure.”

“Sure, if you like the muscle-bound type. I mean, he was okay, you know, in that way. But I thought you were pretty cute. I used to stare when you weren’t looking.”

“Ha,” he said, embarrassed.

“Oh, look now, he’s blushing!”

“Okay, okay,” Roy said, feeling how red his face had become.

“So, really, how have you been, Roy?”

“Not bad. Working at the Point. Thinking about going back to Essex CC. I don’t know. Seems like the time for making changes.” Dina straddling him flashed into his mind, her breasts startlingly white against her tan. He took a long, slow breath.

“Yeah, I’m the same,” she said. “Not about school. Had enough of that. I’m selling women’s clothes at Hutzler’s. It’s okay if you like working in a department store. I don’t know what’s next. Something better. I was seeing this guy—you wouldn’t know him, from Towson—but that kind of fell apart a few weeks back, so...”

He waited to see if she was going to go on. She drifted into her own thoughts for a moment. “Oh, I meant to say before—sorry about you and Della. I heard you broke up. Right? I mean...”

“We did. Not what I wanted. She gave me the ‘We need to see other people’ speech and that was all she wrote.”

“Oh, that’s so sad. You guys seemed like the perfect couple.”

He shrugged.

"Well, don't get down about it. There's plenty of girls who would like to be with you, believe me."

"Maybe."

"No 'maybe,' Mr. Modest. For sure."

"We'll see. The same's true for you, though, right? Gotta beat 'em away with a stick."

"That is so sweet," she said and leaned forward, kissing him on the cheek. He expected her to sit back again but she stayed there, her breath whispering against his face, alcohol scented.

"Aw, he's shy," she said. "Are you shy?"

He didn't answer. She eased his face toward hers and kissed his lips. He didn't respond. She kissed him again more forcefully. He let his mouth go soft against hers, then open. He could taste the punch.

Her hand circled his neck caressing him as her breath became more insistent.

He slipped his hand around her bare waist, rubbing her lower back, feeling the knobs of her spine, the soft dunes of her hips. She kissed him more heatedly.

"Roy," she said, squeezing his upper arms, raking lightly along his back with her hard nails. She was kissing his face then back to his mouth. She scooted forward, drawing him tightly, her breasts against his arm. He felt his stomach grow hot and tense, his skin prickle with the kind of flame that had seized him with Angela.

A voice in his head was telling him to go, just get away, but a louder one was shouting over it: "Go on, man, do it! She's begging for it. Get that god damn condom out and do it, hell with everything, just go for it!"

And he did, quickly pushing his hand up under her top to grasp her bare breast.

In an instant she was pulling back from him, slapping at his face and head with both hands, setting his ears to ringing. He yanked his hand free and leapt from the bed.

“You ignorant fuck!” she yelled, pursuing him, slapping at him continually, landing hard.

“Whoa, whoa, whoa,” he shouted. “What are you doing? You were all like—“ But he didn’t finish as she came at him now with hands extended toward his face, trying to get those flashing red nails into him. He ducked away as best he could, dashing onto the balcony.

“He attacked me,” she screeched as she followed him out. “Get him!”

Her face was purple; her voice a siren howl.

He backed into several guys. They grabbed hold of him and immediately started pummeling as if they’d just been waiting for a signal.

He couldn’t find his voice to protest, fists were hitting him all over his face and body. He collapsed into a protective fetal position on the floor, Kimberly still screaming down at him.

“You creep! Pervert! Get him out of here!”

The fists stopped suddenly. He felt relieved, then suddenly he was being lifted. He struggled violently but now it seemed that the whole party had their hands on him.

“Listen,” he panted, “no, wait, listen, listen!”

A fist blasted his mouth into a bloody torrent.

“Let’s throw him over,” someone said with a hoarse laugh.

He wriggled madly again, hoping to god against that.

“Nah, that’ll bring the fuzz; let’s baptize the fucker,” another said.

“Just get him away from me,” Kimberly shouted.

They were going down the steps. Carrying him like a corpse, like it was all a big joke now, whooping like Indians.

Down to the street level porch. Across the boardwalk. Out onto the sand.

And dropped him face down at the water’s edge with a splash. Laughing and cursing at him, they went away.

He lay still for a while. A swift rush of cold water under his legs told him to crawl up on the beach before the tide came in further. He pulled himself forward on his belly only to stop at a pair of bare feet with bright red toenails.

Kimberly knelt down in the sand. “Jesus, man, you’re a real mess.”

“Yeah.”

“I don’t feel sorry for you.”

“Okay,” he said.

“I just wanted a make-out session, you jerk. Della told me you were a really good kisser.”

What could he say to that? Della; Christ.

“And maybe you are,” she continued, “but you don’t respect girls, that’s for damn sure.”

She knelt there, looking at him. It was too much effort to lift his head and look up. What was there to see, anyway? He turned his head to one side and rested it on his arms. He listened to the ocean so close behind him.

She was still there. What did she want?

“Kimberly?”

“What?”

“Could you just go away now?”

“Sure, no problem, you asshole. Just wanted to make sure you weren’t dead, though I don’t know why I’d care.” She got up, brushing the sand from her knees. She started to turn then crouched down in front of him. “You know what? Forget asshole. Nah, what you are? You are a total piece of shit. Total.”

“Thanks,” he said, meaning it, knowing she wouldn’t get it.

“Oh, Jesus Mary and Joseph,” she said. “Fuck you.” He watched her striding away, burning into a silhouette against the blaze of the setting sun.

Roy rolled over onto his back. The rush of water under his legs was soothing; he didn’t want to move, didn’t want to test just yet to see if anything was broken.

The sky just above the ocean was easing into a soft purplish gray. Higher up it had started to darken and he thought he could see some stars piercing through.

He tasted the blood now as it leaked into his throat.

“Thanks,” he said again.

8

STAG

A week later, physical damage healing, Roy's psyche was still in tatters. The whole thing with Kimberly was like going into a fun house mirror room and seeing all his relationships in a thousand repeating images. He couldn't figure out why things always seemed to get royally screwed up but there was no doubt he was in the center of all the reflections

All that was left was to move on. And to stay away from females for the time being. Far away.

It was mid-August. School, if he chose that route, would be starting up in a few weeks, right after Labor Day. It seemed like a good idea but then so did having a salary and doing what he felt like, mostly on his own terms.

School meant courses in stuff he wasn't interested in—homework, having to show up for classes on a regular basis if he wanted to pass, however minimally.

What he really needed from school might not even be possible, he reflected. If he'd had to write an essay about it, he would have titled it "Wanted: Something Better." What he lacked most was a sense of how to live. It was that simple: how to exist on clear terms without constantly falling into conflict and craziness.

At least I know this, he thought. I have some basic clue, like there's this road sign a hundred miles away I can't see yet but I know it's there. But how the hell to get close enough?

He sensed that it would take a serious immersion in what was going on in the worlds of books, art, film, music—everything that was emerging with an energy that was irresistible. He wanted to move to France after seeing Truffaut's The 400 Blows and Agnès Varda's Cléo from 5 to 7 at a festival. How do people know how to tell a story so painfully honest like that, he wondered. Hell, how do they know it's okay to even try?

At the same time, the "British Invasion" just kept coming like a tidal wave. The Beatles had unlocked a door and a dozen other bands came bursting through, all sounding so different from American music and now, for him, much cooler than the Beach Boys. "Little Surfer Girl" couldn't hold a candle now to the Rolling Stones' "Little Red Rooster," a blues song full of menace and exciting guitar licks. He longed to be inside that music somehow, know it, learn its secrets, drink its essence.

Books new to him—One Flew Over the Cuckoo's Nest, Hot Water Music, A Confederate General from Big Sur— were piled on his bedside table, whispering about other worlds.

There was, he sensed, this string that ran through the universe, vibrating from the voices of all these creators. He could hear the sound of it, feel the communion of it, something rising up in luminosity and color: music, art, writing, movies, a tidal wave steadily building to catch and ride forever.

He wanted it all and there it was, a giant delectable buffet calling to him.

And then there was work. The steel mill, grinding on him daily like a pencil being over-sharpened.

He remembered seeing the silent film Metropolis at Essex CC and felt exactly like one of the mindless minions in dreary lockstep: punch in, do the same thing every day, punch out, sit in the vapor that trailed out of the day of work, numbed, futureless. He could finally understand why the first stop out of the mill for a lot of guys was the nearest bar.

He didn't need to fall into that. There was a sort of graduation parade that had been going on in front of his eyes: guys drifting steadily from the Arundel corner to Coleman's bar down the street, going from milk shakes to boilermakers—boys turning rapidly into gray old men. Was there anything beyond that, then? Or just other bars? Was it just twenty-one-and-you're-done?

It sent a chill through him to think of people steadily marinating through their days.

He didn't know how to think it all through. He didn't have to go to some local joint when he was already comfortable and accepted at Martick's downtown. Drinking there—watching the shifting weave of local artists and street loonies, listening to jazz, talking with whoever felt like a momentary friendship—was an adventure, not surrender. There, at least, he could sit in a corner and read.

Doing that in a bar in Dundalk was to invite a lot of commentary, if not invasion. He had never figured out why being smart and bookish was offensive to some people.

Work. School. Seesaw shifting.

In a way, none of it really mattered enough for him to lean this way or that. It was hard to focus. The loss of Dina was growing into an elephant to carry about as the days squandered themselves.

He concocted a thousand plans. Fretfully revisited the events of the break-up, looking for some glimmer that could reverse it. This was far worse, he knew, than the whole thing with Della or with previous relationships. This was the love of his life he'd blown it with.

He tried to put it behind him but it had simply climbed onto his back

He ached to jump in his car and drive down the Ocean and yet he knew he absolutely couldn't risk it. Not only because of Dina but to stay away from how crazy it made him to be there.

Kimberly sputtered through his thoughts for a second with her insistent tongue, big breasts and blood red nails. He shivered at the recollection.

There were moments, hours, when he promised himself he'd never go back down the Ocean ever again, swearing to all that was holy to avoid it at all costs. But it wouldn't let him go, pestering him like a mosquito. He finally promised himself not to go back until next summer. And even after a year-long break he'd need to be leery of the memories and mistakes.

He was wandering around Eastpoint mall one afternoon, killing time before heading down the Point for a 3-11 shift, when he ran into Dougie Grafton, a high school classmate.

Grafton was somebody he had avoided back at Dundalk high. One of those guys without a filter, always braying on about some nonsense, laughing at his own jokes and ever confident that he was the coolest cat of them all.

Roy immediately noticed how much hair Grafton had lost already and how much weight he'd put on in just over a year. He looked forty years old.

"Newson!" came the jackass bellow.

Roy was tempted to dive into a store but it was too late.

"Hey, Grafton."

"Yeah, great, hey. So how's it hangin' there, buddy?"

"Everything's peachy dandy."

Grafton spluttered with laughter. "Peachy dandy!" he shouted. "Jesus Christ if you ain't still a pisser. Who talks like that? 'Peachy dandy,' that's a fuckin' pisser. So, what are you up to?"

Drunk and sweaty Nancy leered at him from behind Grafton's eyes, echoing "Peachy dandy!" Roy blinked her away. "Ah, you know. Working down the Point. Watching it all go by."

"Yeah, man, I know that tune for sure. I'm still at McCormick. Yeah, steady work."

McCormick's was a spice processing plant located downtown off the harbor. Roy liked going by the place for its exotic aromas. Even so, Grafton somehow always smelled like armpit.

"I thought you was at Essex," Grafton continued.

"Yeah, I was there for a bit. Might go back."

"Weighin' the old options, huh?"

"Yep." Roy held his arms out like a balance scale and tipped from side to side.

Grafton hooted and clapped his hands. "Ha, man, that's a good one. Oh, hey, you heard about Camber?"

Roy blanched for a moment, thinking this was something about Angela.

"Heard what?"

"Flunked out of them redeemable courses there at Merlin," he said, mangling Maryland with his accent.

"No, really? Damn, that's too bad." Roy decided not to point out the difference between remedial and redeemable—though maybe they weren't so far apart anyway.

"That ain't the whole story. Fucker joined the Army. I mean, I didn't know whether to shit or go blind when I heard that."

"The Army? Wow. Really?" Roy was genuinely flabbergasted.

"Yep. Weird, ain't it? I for sure saw him in the Marines."

Roy chuckled. There was rarely a same page to be on with Grafton. "Well, that he joined any branch of the service is what I mean. Why the hell did he do that?"

Grafton looked around for a moment, as if they were in some cross-hairs. "You remember Ike Colombini? Graduated, what, Sixty-One?"

"Vaguely."

"Well, Ike joined up and they sent him to this place called Veet-nam. He come back on leave last week and me and Camber and a couple of guys ran into him at Harold's bar. Ike says there's something going on there, like, they're talkin' about bringin' more guys over and gettin' into it with the Chinks. Some bullshit in some bay there, Tonka or somethin' like that. Ike says the draft is going to heat up. So Camber, I think he was still shit-faced, goes out the next mornin' and signs up."

Roy shook his head. "Jesus. Camber. In the Army."

"Yeah, huh? Can't wait until he comes home after Basic, man. I gotta see that big stud bastard without all that fuckin' hair of his."

Roy laughed out loud. Picturing Phil without his perfect pompadour was hilarious, no two ways about it.

"Well, sign me up for that viewing, for sure." Roy laughed again.

"Yeah," Grafton said. He turned serious: "Look, I'm just sayin' this because you're one of those guys could be okay. Get back in school. I mean it. Ike says all the officers and NCOs he was around were talking how the draft is going to go gang busters. People are pissed. This little turd bowl country—fuckin' who even knows where it is—and they start shootin' at our boats and shit? So, yeah, Uncle Sam's got his eye on you, buddy, believe it. Maybe I'm lucky after all with this. 4-F, baby."

He pulled up his pants leg, revealing grotesque scars on his calf. Roy had forgotten: both of Grafton's legs had been badly burned in a house fire when Grafton was a kid.

"First time I ever thought about thanking my step-father for anything. Drunk cocksucker."

Roy nodded. What was there to say back to that?

He had no clue how to think about anything Grafton was going on about. Everybody signed up at 18 for the "Selective Service," but now it was starting to shape itself into something actual, like that letter saying "Greetings" from Uncle Sam could arrive any day.

More time floated by on Grafton's river of commentary and then they were shaking hands and heading in opposite directions. He watched the guy walk away with his jiggety limp, rocking side to side like a metronome.

Driving home he started thinking about the military thing. Is that something he wanted to do? Not wait but just join up? Didn't seem likely. He'd seen enough war movies to know that even basic training would be likely to wipe him out, let alone face down enemy bullets. Still, maybe it could get him out of the rut he was falling into in Baltimore, start over, shake off this rotten summer.

But it couldn't be Army or Marines. No, he looked better in blue, so Navy or Air Force. Roy laughed at himself: such an idiot.

Full-time students weren't subject to the draft: that was worth thinking about for sure, rather than something as heart-sinking as getting shot at, dying in some nowhere country.

When he got to work that afternoon, there was a sign on the bulletin board: "Stag Party in Honor of Chester's Retirement." The date was the coming Saturday. Roy had no clue what a stag party might be. It didn't matter—he wasn't planning to go. Parties were not where he wanted to be right now.

Chester was an okay old guy, in Roy's view. He did the time sheets and other reports for the office. He was a sweet character, bald as a dinosaur egg, not much of a talker. Roy had no idea if the guy was married or not, had kids or not. He was just part of the office furniture.

Roy went into the locker room to change for his shift. Simmons, the jerk who told everybody dirty things about his wife, was sitting on the bench tying his shoes.

"What ho," Simmons said in what Roy guessed was supposed to be an English accent. "Here cometh the relief shift."

"Yup," Roy said.

"Can't wait to get home. Mama's cooking up something hot for me. And probably some food, too." Simmons reared back, hee-hawing at his own joke. Roy hoped he'd fall backwards and break his stupid head open.

"Guess you saw the notice, huh, Roy?"

"What—about the party?"

"No, the one says you're fired." Simmons brayed again. "Yes, the fucking party, man!"

"Yeah, I saw it."

"Good."

"Why is that good?" Roy asked, all blink-eyed innocence. He wasn't going to give the creep an inch.

"Why? Because it's a party and it's for good old Chester. You're coming, right?"

"Doubt it. Too late to get a date."

"Date? This here is a stag party, buddy. Men only, no chicks. Aw, come on, you're pullin' my leg, you knew that already, right?"

"Sure," Roy mumbled, hoping not to blush.

"Aw, sure, yeah, you big jokester you. Okay, well, I'm off until Monday, so I'll see you at the soiree," he said rhyming the last syllable with bee.

"Yeah, no, probably not."

"Oh, come on, you gotta. This is one of those things you just gotta do."

"I'll think about it."

"Attaboy. Okay, then, home to the little woman. She'll be pantin' for it by now."

Simmons gave his crotch a hoist, then left the room. Roy could feel all the bullshit trailing out the door with him. The whole space heaved a sigh.

After that encounter he most certainly didn't want any part of the gathering. Toward the end of his shift he saw his boss, Ed Eakins, waddling his way across the plant floor. The guy was so enormous his hard hat sat atop his head like a marshmallow.

"Oh, hey, Newson. I saw Simmons when I come in. Says you might not show for Chester."

"Ahh, I don't know, Ed. I mean, I'm the newest guy here—I don't really have any kind of ties to Chester."

"This ain't a 'I don't know' thing, kid. You're comin'."

"I don't get what the big deal is."

"The big deal is that I want one hundred percent representation at this party. We owe it to him. Sign of respect. Every man on board to wave old Chester out the door, get me?"

"Am I going to get fired if I don't come?"

"Of course not."

Roy nodded, thinking they were done.

"No, you're going to get double shifts two or three times a week for the next month is what you're going to get."

Roy looked at the guy for a moment, his flat shark-like eyes pegged into a pink sea of meat.

"Well, then," Roy said, fetching up his finest lackey smile, "what can I bring to the party?"

For the remainder of his shift, Roy thought about going over Eakins' head to the general foreman but threw the notion away. Bitching about a supervisor wasn't small potatoes. Guys got fired for trivial crap all the time and this would be bigger than that. He was pretty bulletproof, given his father's status in the mills, but that didn't mean he had a totally free ride.

And anyway, if he ratted out Eakins, his dad would be sure to get a call. Things at home had finally settled a bit after Roy had blown off those few days to see Dina. He didn't need all the hassle.

On Saturday, he drove to the party on 33rd Street near North Charles Street in the city. It was an area he loved, close to Johns Hopkins University and Memorial Stadium where the Orioles and the Colts played. Some of the buildings in the area were huge: mostly apartment complexes, packed with Hopkins students. He enviously imagined their lifestyles: true college people whose lives were on a perpetual intellectual crusade in profound study of a thousand great mysteries.

The building for the party was set back from the street a bit. It took him a few minutes to spot the number and then realized that cars were end to end all along the block. He finally nabbed a spot when somebody pulled out.

The street door was wide open. The party was on the top floor, Eakins had told him: five flights up, no elevator. Roy started the long climb. He noticed odors coming from all directions. There were foreign cooking smells he couldn't identify but was intrigued by. He'd had Chinese food but this was different—more pungent and sharp, maybe Indian? He wanted to go knocking on doors to beg for tastes. Somebody was cooking cabbage, a sour aroma that was way too familiar from his mother's cooking. Elsewhere he could identify burgers or maybe steaks being grilled. Throughout the stairwells the cooking mixed with a mustiness that signaled city life to him: old wood, dust, uncountable dwellers having moved through.

When he arrived at the apartment, the door was open and the party was in full throat. Eakins had certainly made sure that attendance was 100% –it was standing room only in the living room, with some guys spilled over into a tiny kitchen. Roy nodded his way through to everyone as he went to shake Chester's hand and make sure that Eakins saw he was there.

Somebody stuck a bottle of beer in his hand. He stood to the side, watching and sipping. Chester was tucked into the corner of a sofa, beaming away, looking somewhere between angelic and moronic, clearly in his cups. People kept going over to him, shaking his hand, saying things to him. Chester kept nodding his head up and down so persistently, Roy wondered where the string was. Eakins took up the rest of the sofa with his mass, his face red and bloated, tie askew.

Out of nowhere a woman appeared and the talk hushed. She was small, dainty, pretty in a worn way. She smiled vaguely around the room until finally spying Simmons. She leaned into him with a peck on his cheek and then departed.

Roy felt sick. This was the woman that Simmons talked about in the crude way he did? This was their apartment? He shook his head to clear it. His eyes flicked from one guy to another as they all watched her exit. He knew, he could see, what they were thinking, all speculating about what was true or not from Simmons' stories. A rush of pity for her raced through him; he ached to get out of there.

He moved along the wall toward the windows. High above a mirror on the other side of the room was a large crucifix surrounded by old family pictures. All the women looked haggard; the men looked cretinous. The beer taste in his mouth turned putrid as he stood looking out to the street below. Mrs. Simmons emerged onto the sidewalk and turned toward North Charles Street. He noticed she'd put on short white gloves on her way down the stairs. Another woman pulled up in a boxy-looking car he didn't recognize and tooted the horn once. Mrs. Simmons waved and got in.

Keep going, he thought. Escape from this asshole.

Roy tried not to look at his watch too often. It wasn't easy, given how he was feeling—careening between anxious and bored. He had no idea if there was some kind of peak event that he needed to stick around for—a cake, dancing girls, something that said "Oh, whoopie-doo, Chester, now go away and be history."

He was just starting to edge toward the door when Simmons appeared from another room, rolling a small cart with a film projector on it.

Oh, great, Roy thought, home movies?

"Okay, guys," Simmons said. "The old lady's out for the evening—just like I ordered her to be," he paused for the laugh. "S-o-o-o here we go. Ta-daaa!"

There was a hubbub of excited reactions and the men began finding places to sit, on chairs and even on the floor. Eakins wasn't about to make way for anyone else except Chester on the couch, that much was evident.

Simmons was pulling the window shades down while someone flipped the lights off.

Standing at the projector, Simmons turned it on and brilliant light shot out. "Let's not have any accidents, fellas," he said, with a wink. He flipped a switch and the film began to roll.

Swatches of black and white jittered across the screen, the projector chattering away, then plain white with droves of scratches and finally a title: “Aunt Jolly’s Sunny Day.”

Roy snorted to himself. What a stupid title. What the hell is this?

And then the film became images in slightly out of focus black and white. A woman wearing a pair of overalls, cut very high on the leg and with no shirt underneath, was watering a garden with a hose. For a moment she struggled to pull the hose forward, then reached way behind her and brought her hand back in view grasping a man’s erect penis. She turned to the camera and mouthed “Oh, my!”

The room erupted in cheers and laughter.

Roy watched, stunned, as the film continued into the couple having sex on a pile of hay in the yard. There was no sound, just the image of the woman’s legs waving bug-like in the air and the pale ass of the man pumping away. Roy felt very uncomfortable as he watched, embarrassed and angry at being there. Now he knew what a “stag” party was.

The film ended abruptly. The men cheered and clapped. Another film started up immediately, in very grainy black and white. A different couple was in what looked like a hotel room. Both wore black masks.

“I edited all these into one long film myself,” Simmons informed the crowd. No one responded; all eyes were glued to the screen. The room had grown very quiet in between the moments of cheering or laughing. Roy was starting to sweat through his shirt, feeling more and more desperate to get out of there.

He crouched down and started easing slowly through the crowd, stopping to sit for a bit, moving again, always inching toward the door. He hoped Eakins wouldn’t see him trying to leave and make a big scene about it. It looked like Eakins might have nodded off but that didn't matter—he was definitely leaving.

As he crept through the assorted men, he took in the faces of those watching the films. Their expressions were either blank, bug-eyed or wolfishly leering. He had never really looked at these guys very closely before. What he saw were working men with sallow skin and aging bodies whose idea of fun was a night like this or playing poker or going to a ball game together. Men spending time with men, away from family, out of view from their wives, getting to do forbidden things like watching these films or losing big at the table, coming home barfing, no distance from who they had been in high school.

He saw his father in a flash, blue collar like these guys, up from hardscrabble streets, old and paunchy too soon, nothing ahead but the days of work and the repetition of work only broken up by a meeting or an accident. "No accidents for X days in 1964." X days, a thousand days, a week, fill in the blank. Where was there any relief in that, for anyone?

Roy felt an awareness growing in him: what his dad was like, why he was like he was. The long, Polonius-like sessions about "When I was your age..." became crystalized: this is what I survived, he was saying—I hope you won't have to. His father could easily be one of the men sitting there, ogling and trying to hide their physical reactions to the films.

He had moved through the room enough to get near the door but the problem was how to open the door and make his escape. He glanced over his shoulder to see yet another film beginning, this time with a naked woman leading a very large dog into a bedroom. He definitely didn't want to see what was going to happen next, especially as an expectant murmur was insinuating its way around the walls.

A door across the hallway slammed and immediately banged back open. A male voice was shouting something in a language that was guttural and harsh. Another voice answered back and a scuffle broke out. Roy seized his chance, leapt to the door and went into the hallway shouting: "Hey, now, come on, break it up, break it up!"

The fighters, two small, dark-complected men, immediately stopped, looking chagrinned. Roy stayed in the hallway, quickly pulling the door shut behind him.

"What's going on, fellas?" he asked in a too-loud voice.

One of the men started explaining in English so rapid and tongue-rolled Roy couldn't begin to follow it.

"Well, now," he said, when the man had run out of breath. "It's Saturday night. Don't wreck it, end up in jail."

That got their attention. One of the men nodded and started back into the other apartment. He stopped and extended his hand to Roy. While they were shaking hands the other man edged by, muttering something under his breath in his language, giving Roy a serious hairy eyeball. Roy didn't care. Both men were short and scrawny; he could have tied them into a bow with ease.

The door to their apartment closed and Roy went down, two and three stairs at a time, racing out of the building.

It took him a minute to remember where the car was. He jumped in and headed toward North Charles Street, deciding to drive away from the city. He loved the long passage from downtown out to the suburbs. The houses along the drive were elegant and spoke to him of a long-gone era.

He glanced in the rear-view mirror to make sure Eakins hadn't charged out after him waving a saber or something. He could just make out Memorial Stadium in the distance behind him, looking abandoned with the Orioles on a road trip.

Maybe this is why he loved the area, he reflected: the stadium. In a profound way it was the only place of connection with his dad.

Starting in 1957, when Roy was 12, they had begun going to the Colts games at Memorial stadium. Getting season tickets was a matter of inheritance for the most part, so his father bought some dreadful bleacher seats in the end zone, in front of the scoreboard, where the game looked flattened out like a Mercator map. But they didn't sit in those after the first time. Instead, they climbed all the way to the very top of the second tier and stood in the space behind the last row.

Roy loved it, spending at least part of the time gazing out from the height at the view of the buildings around the stadium. When cold or inclement weather set in, watching a game was an endurance test. His father brought cardboard for them to stand on above the frigid concrete and they bundled up so fully Roy could barely move his arms. His father's buddy from work, Joe, brought food for them, packed cleverly by his wife: mustard swiped buns with a layer of chopped onions packed in wax paper and piping hot chicken broth in a thermos with Polish sausages floating inside to go on the buns. Eat the dogs, drink the soup, breathe in the stadium melange of smells, listen to the fans all around.

With the Colts they lived and died, Sunday after Sunday, at the stadium or in front of the television. It was the only place and situation where Roy felt comfortable with his father. There they could talk about anything other than what-was-wrong-with-Roy, embrace each other jumping up and down over a miraculous play, savor the wins and commiserate over losses.

In '58, when the Colts beat the hated New York Giants in the first overtime championship game ever played, life was tinged with brilliance, especially after dozens of nail-biting moments. The seesaw battle ending in a tie was bad enough, but during the overtime, somebody disconnected the TV cable in Yankee stadium. Roy and his father nearly knocked each other down racing for the kitchen radio, only to find the TV broadcast back on quickly. They stood there, breathless and nearly paralyzed with hope and fear, then deliriously celebrated the winning moment, leaping about like wild beasts.

Roy and his dad were best buddies for weeks afterwards, talking endlessly about the game and Alan Ameche's plunge across the goal line to win. Life was perfect around the house until Roy failed an important test and then it was back to variations on The Talk, with long months to go until football season came around again.

He didn't know what it was about him that his father found so frustrating. Through his entire experience of public school, Roy had never been more than an average student. He didn't care much about any of it and felt that his dad ought to share that. Hell, Dad only got to the 8th grade—why does he always bug me so much?

His mom was different in that. She often said to him, "Roy, I don't care if you end up a truck driver, so long as you're happy." He tried not to feel a bit insulted at her choice of career for him but he knew what she meant. When she looked at him she didn't see a failure.

But it was mostly what his dad seemed to see.

As he drove along North Charles, he kept coming back to the same thing. He wanted a father like the TV fathers he saw being patient and wise. He longed to ask his father: what does it mean to be a man? Based on the roller coaster summer of '64 he felt more clueless than ever.

But after what he'd just seen at the party, he thought maybe he knew one answer: don't be like men you don't respect and who don't respect anyone else, don't settle for a lifetime of eating shit from guys like Eakins or fossilizing in some dingy office like poor old Chester.

He drove around for a long while, pondering everything he'd experienced at the party. It was very late when he got home.

He tiptoed in as quietly as he could, then realized the stove light was on in the kitchen. This usually meant some treat left for him by his mother but when he passed through the doorway he realized his father was sitting at the table

“Dad?”

“Hey, Roy.”

“What are you doing up? It’s, like, two a.m. Everything okay?”

“Yeah.” His father let that hang for a moment. “You go to that party?”

Roy felt himself flush. How did his father know about the party? Well, how would he not? It wasn’t like the steel mill was an isolation booth.

“Yeah, I was there for about twenty minutes, but I hated it so I split.”

“That so?”

“Scout’s honor,” Roy said, hoping for a smile.

“Good, then. I didn’t know was I supposed to tell you what it was or not, if you already knew or not.”

“I didn’t. Made me sick, dad, no kidding.”

“You understand why I wouldn’t go to something like that myself.”

“Yeah, for sure. Jeez, I wouldn’t’ve thought you ever did.”

“Everybody was young once, Roy.”

“That’s true,” Roy said, now unhappily confronted with the image of his dad as a kid at a stag party. He didn’t know how to respond to that at all.

Silence slipped into the room, into his mom’s kitchen. Everything felt tainted.

“Okay,” his father said after a moment, getting up. “Okay.”

He started to leave the kitchen but stopped in front of Roy, looking up at him. Roy had long since become a head taller than his father. They locked eyes for a split second, then his dad nodded and scuffed away in his slippers.

Roy watched him go, mystified as always by their encounters.

He raided the fridge for the green grapes his mother had bought that morning. They were so cold and delicious he wanted to eat them all but managed to stop himself halfway.

He sat at the table for a while longer, listening to the fridge hum and the tiny noises the house made at night.

He was amazed that his father hadn't made him sit down for yet another variation of The Talk. Then a thought struck him. After all, what could his dad have said? "Well, son, back when I went to dirty movies..."

Roy chuckled. His father had waited up, having no angle on The Talk, to see what Roy had to say for once. It was amazing. He shivered.

Roy looked around the kitchen, his mother's domain. He thought about all the times after school, sitting there with her and chatting about the day while she worked on putting supper together. He always felt better talking to her. Felt more at ease, anyway, knowing she was less likely to judge him.

Now he felt like an intruder, a reverse thief bringing vileness into this world. He cursed himself for giving in to attending the party. A deep sense of shame curled into his gut like an invading parasite taking hold.

Images from the stag films streamed across his mind. He wondered if he'd ever see women the same way again. Did everything boil down to the level of Angela or to braggart Simmons and whatever journey his wife was on?

What are we to one another, guys and girls? If Dina and I had made love, would I still feel the same about her? Would she have smelled as bad as Angela did? Do we call it making love when we just mean screwing? Tab A, Slot A. What the fuck am I supposed to do or think or feel about any of this?

He clenched his fist so hard and tight his arm was shaking. He brought it down sharply, stopping just above the table's surface, wanting to bash straight through, holding off against needless noise, pointless damage.

Choices, he thought. Choices.

Early on Monday, Roy drove to the mill, walked into the office and placed his hard hat on Eakins' desk.

"What's this?" the fat man asked.

“I quit.”

“What, just like that? That ain’t right. How am I supposed to replace you without any notice?”

“Not my problem, Ed. I start school right after Labor Day and I’m taking my vacation days now. Oh, and my dad already knows so you can skip the phone call.”

Ed’s mouth opened, then closed.

Roy smiled and walked away.

9

NEW YEAR

Roy was sitting atop a railing, looking out at the gray, seething Atlantic.

The beach was empty but for a few walkers and the proverbial guy with a metal detector.

December 31st, 1964, he thought. New Year's eve. Holy shit. Long way from July—from any July ever, it seemed.

He was cold. The perennial wind along the boardwalk carried the sea with it like an inside current, icing the air, even though the temperature was around fifty degrees. The sky was a long gray sheet of steel.

Roy had driven down in the morning, not wanting to be home with a party in full preparation. It would be his parents' friends—mostly guys his dad worked with at Sparrows Point and their wives—all nice people but prone to get louder and shriller by the drink. Roy hated being around drunken behavior, everyone red-faced and careening, couldn't stand the reek of alcohol and cigarettes closing in on him. The memory of being ganged up on and the whole Kimberly thing hadn't left him, nor had the stag party.

He couldn't understand the behavior of older people. In some ways his parents' generation made sense, having gone through the Depression and the second world war. They'd been into places he hadn't. But the people he had worked with at the Point—some were only one generation ahead of him—what made them so messed up? He didn't get it. He only wanted to avoid it, whatever it was. That definitely included parties of all stripes.

Various old friends, now returned from college or on leave, had called him up, invited him to this or that. He'd longed to reconnect through the summer but the idea of mixing it up in somebody's club basement now just felt like pure claustrophobia. He still carried too much from the Angela party. He put them off, saying it would be great to meet another day over a beer or coffee.

What he wanted was quiet. Peace. Respite from all these crowding memories.

And Dina. He still wanted Dina with such an ache in his being there were times when he didn't think he could get through another day without going crazy.

A few weeks after the stag night Roy had started writing letters to Dina. The whole event, the raw sex on the screen, the rapt attention of the men in the room, had deeply unnerved him. And he'd seen something in the way Mrs. Simmons looked when she exited the party—so much older than her years. Something told him that maybe Simmons wasn't entirely exaggerating about how he used her. He didn't know what that might mean to her, only that she looked like a candle at low flicker.

What about love, he wondered. What about the thing that makes two people turn into one being?

And what about now—being only half of something that doesn't even exist any more? What's half of zero?

He wanted Dina back. He wrote without self-censoring or trying to paint himself with any brush but a true one. He told her he understood how horribly he'd behaved and how he wanted to make it up somehow. He apologized, berated himself without mercy, pledged a lifetime of complete truthfulness and faithfulness. Anything she wanted from him, he would do. Anything.

He feared the letters would come flying back. None did. That seemed like a good sign. But then she wasn't responding, either. He debated many times about just showing up at her parents' house or at Salisbury State, saying: "Here I am, please take me back."

He would have done it but for the horrifying movie that loomed up with images of her screaming at him or one of her family members getting violent.

"If you want, I will fall on my knees and beg," he wrote in several of the letters. No gesture of remorse was too low for him to undertake. He even considered doing radical things to get her attention. Cutting his face and sending a photo of that to her. Carving her initials into his arm deep enough to scar.

He wasn't about to hack off an ear but many other self-punishments skittered through his mind during the months of nights he endured, sleepless and overwrought.

He was grateful for the late night jazz shows on the local radio. One came on after midnight: "The Harley Show," hosted by some guy who owned sandwich shops around Baltimore. Roy loved the man's growly voice and deep knowledge of jazz. Harley often sounded like he was pretty well along into a bottle and that was okay with Roy so long as he didn't have to be in the room with the guy. They kept company most nights until 2 a.m., when the show signed off and the radio fell to static.

But since the disaster, Harley and even the magical station from Chicago brought no help. Silence became his companion as he listened to the blood whispering in his veins, while the house ticked and grumbled through the interminable nights.

He plunged more deeply into reading, looking for answers, but the books he encountered—Catch-22, Revolutionary Road, Big Sur—only succeeded in deepening his confusion about women and relationships. It seemed as if absolutely no one could figure this stuff out. Well, his parents, maybe, though there were many times he had the feeling they were just animated mannequins with their real selves buried too deep to ever re-emerge.

What did it come down to, then? Be like Phil Camber, chasing just about every girl he saw? Or like so many of his graduating class: get married, have babies, get socked in—house, car, retirement plan...death.

It wasn't what he wanted, deep in his guts. There was some something, unnamable, invisible, that he knew was there —but it remained untouchable.

All that was left was the tightrope he walked, balanced between fear and hope, no net below.

If he could just get through to Dina, maybe the answer was with her. At moments he felt certain it was. When they were together, when it was still good, it didn't need to be discussed or dissected. They shared the something he longed for—they made a third person between them, one that could see ahead with clarity, that wasn't afraid all the time of what could go wrong or how it might be seen, judged, by others.

He wrote letter after letter. Most were composed and rewritten many times over in his mind as he gazed at the ceiling.

His letters starting in mid-December were different. He needed to move beyond mere words. Each ended with the same lines: "Please meet me at Thirteenth and Boardwalk, New Year's Eve. I'll be there from four until midnight. I want to apologize in person and start the new year off better, if you'll let me. Just let me tell you I'm sorry to your face. It's all I want."

There was no rhyme or reason to the choice of place, except maybe tempting the fates with the number thirteen. He really harbored no hope of getting back together, though some part of him was always leaning toward her.

Regardless, he had a bottom line: he wanted to be forgiven, cleansed.

On the 31st he drove down the Ocean in silence, a fifth of whiskey by his side, the fields looking blasted now, no hint of the summer's green riot.

The streets were nearly deserted as he drove through and pulled up near the rendezvous place. He felt like a character in a Twilight Zone episode—the last man on earth. He got out of the car and walked to the boardwalk, smiling at the first moment of taking in the ocean, and then settled on the rail to wait.

I'll be here until midnight, he thought. And she won't come.

Roy shivered and lit another cigarette. He slipped down from the rail, landing with a jolt on the hardened sand. He walked, hands in his jacket pockets, wind whipping his hair. He went to the water's edge, turned and ambled along until he came to where he could see Twelfth Street, then reversed course to the end of the other block, keeping an eye on the meeting spot. Back and forth, the wind scudding sea foam into ghost ships across his path.

"Why am I such an idiot?" he asked the sky.

He flicked his cigarette out into the ocean, watched it bob back toward shore, then retreat again in a tumult of shells and tiny stones dragged by the undertow.

The water had created rivulets in the wet sand, looking like long claw marks, as if the ocean was tearing away at the land, reclaiming it for itself. It was a long process, he realized, the sea gathering the sand into its arms while pulverizing the objects it carried into eventual grains. What was it from Chem class? Entropy and "ord" something. Ordiny—that was it. Jesus, why would he remember those when the formula for salt wouldn't come to mind on the final? Those terms probably weren't right anyway but he liked the way they sounded.

"Entropy," he said aloud.

A knot of young guys startled him, materializing like sand creatures suddenly come to life. They passed, not one looking his way, pounding down the beach like a zany comedy act, heads bobbing at different heights. A high school track team, maybe, he thought. Escapees from a nut house. Who cares?

High school seemed light years behind him. Hell, what didn't?

Roy had gone back to Essex Community College the same day he walked away from the Point. He'd left without a second glance. The job, the shift work, the guys there, that disgusting party—it was all a big zero. He wanted time to explore what his instincts were telling him to do. And he wanted to stay far, far away from the draft because the news about Viet Nam was, indeed, getting more and more worrisome.

Coming back to school was weird after being a working stiff even for just a little while. Many of the students seemed really young to him, aimless and indolent, but it was a soft valley between the possibilities of steel mill shrapnel or enemy fire.

He tried to knuckle down but the gods of elsewhere kept leading him off campus to explore bookstores, galleries and museums, ferreting out downtown bars with lax standards. It didn't matter. So long as he kept a "C" average and stayed full-time, he was safe from the bony hands of Uncle gathering up cannon fodder. He was learning what he needed to, spending monkish weekends in the paired art film houses on North Avenue—the 5 West and the 7 East—with their coffee house atmospheres and pale, cerebral clientele.

Roy suddenly shivered again. It was so cold at the water's edge. He retreated to the boardwalk and found shelter between the empty buildings. Out of the wind he could feel the sun's faint winter warmth.

It was so eerie being down Ocean City at this time of year. Ghost City, more like.

On the drive from Baltimore he'd chased his thoughts in many directions, mostly in Technicolor dreams of Dina accompanied by violins and Disney bluebirds. "Yeah, sure," he said to the mirror.

Going across the Bay Bridge he started thinking about the magnet that being down the Ocean was for him, long before Dina. His parents had preferred Atlantic City when he was a kid. It was okay. The Steel Pier was cool but had absolutely nothing on the parent-free environment of being down the Ocean, where he could run as wild as he pleased.

He remembered a night when he'd been there with some buddies, all of them sixteen and giddy with a shared bottle of vodka, having escaped their keepers on a weekend retreat with some rah-rah-Jesus group.

So much bolder then, he'd stormed into various gaggles of girls along the boardwalk, going straight up to the prettiest one in each group and kissing her before she could react, then dashing off again, laughing savagely. Most reared back in surprise but one girl grabbed hold of him for an extended, open-mouthed kiss that sent him reeling into the night.

Great times, he thought, letting other memories flood in as he sat gazing out at the winter sky, waiting, hoping for Dina. The ceaseless sound of the ocean shushed him as his mind slowly deadened.

Abruptly there was movement nearby. Someone had appeared at the left periphery of his sight, popping out from beside the building, then was gone again. A flash.

Dina.

No?

He waited.

Should he get up and look? Call out her name? Would that spook her? Whoever it was didn't seem to be coming back. Had they seen him? Had she?

Swearing at his stupidity, he leapt up and left his sheltered spot for the boardwalk. Some guy he didn't know came walking out from next to the building, followed a few seconds later by Dina.

Roy froze. His heart a bird battering against its cage.

The guy walked to the railing where Roy had sat earlier and perched there, looking out toward the gray, roiling sea.

Dina stood on the boardwalk, watching Roy, her hair now longer and being kited about by the wind. She looked like a movie star.

"Hi," Roy said, struggling to dredge up some moisture in his mouth.

Dina said nothing.

"Who's that?" Roy asked, trying not to sound as if he thought the guy was Dina's new love.

"My cousin. Merle. He drove." she said. Roy jolted at the sound of her voice, surprised. His elbow began itching like crazy. He scratched at it through the jacket sleeve.

"So, so, so, uh, hey, Dina, how are you?"

"I'm okay," she said. "You?"

"Oh, well, you read all the..." he trailed off.

"Yeah, well, I got 'all the' but I maybe read two or three."

"Sure, yeah, I get that."

"Do you? I mean, seriously, did you think I was going to go running to Baltimore and throw myself in your arms?"

"No."

"Well, what then?"

"What I said over and over. I want to be forgiven."

"Okay," she said, her voice flat. "You're forgiven."

The wind was picking up as the daylight began to shift to a deeper gray. Dina wrapped her arms around herself.

Roy stood there, waiting for her to say more.

"Well, good, then," he said in a mocking way, hoping she couldn't see his disappointment.

She sighed and started to turn toward the guy on the railing.

"Wait," he said, holding his hand out toward her, open-palmed.

"What?"

"Come on, don't 'what' me. I mean, here you are. You took the trouble to drive down the Ocean and here you are and that's it?"

"What do you want, violins? Fireworks?"

Roy reddened. "I don't know," he said, recovering. "I guess I got what I wanted. Feels like a whole lot of not much. Come on: why did you come?"

"I wanted to see you," she said, with a shrug.

"Okay."

"I wanted to be sure, is all. Sure that I remembered you right."

"Okay, so do you?"

"Mostly. Never saw you in long pants and a jacket before, so I guess that's something different."

"Come on, Dina, what's going on?"

She took a breath, then let it out so completely her shoulders slumped and her head dropped forward slightly. She stayed that way, gazing at the weathered planks of the boardwalk. Roy wanted to comfort her. He didn't dare move or speak.

When she lifted her head again her face was streaked.

"I need you," she began, then faltered. His spirits started to lift. "I need you to just let me be, Roy."

"Oh."

"That's really all. I came because I thought if you saw me, really saw me, it might help you to understand how bad you hurt me—"

He started to speak. She waved him off. A bitter taste was gathering at the back of his throat.

"I need you to look at me and realize that you might as well have bashed my head in. That's how bad it was. And all your letters—and okay, I read more than a few because I just kept waiting and praying that one would finally say you were done sticking needles in me."

She barked a sharp humorless laugh.

"So, yeah," she said. "I came so you could look at my face and see what's real and true. That I'm a person and you need to stop all this."

No words formed in his mind. He nodded.

"I don't hate you, Roy, just so you know. I did at the time but not any more. Life's too short for hating. Anyhow I came here because of that but really because it's on the way to a party we're heading up to in Rehoboth."

He felt as if she'd just slapped him. He was losing air, shrinking.

"And," she said, her voice greatly softening, "well, I hoped maybe I could get you to understand something, Roy. Something I didn't want to try to put in a return letter."

"Oh, goody," he said, knowing he sounded like some spoiled kid.

"Okay, fine, never mind," she said, turning again.

"Wait," he said. "Please; I'm sorry."

She stopped. "Are you listening? Because I'm getting cold out here and I don't want to waste my time."

He nodded, unable to catch his breath.

"Maybe you won't get this now but what you had with me, that was unconditional love, Roy. I fell for you so hard. Anything you wanted, needed, I would've given it, pure and simple. If you'd told me you killed JFK, I would've loved you still. Anything. Do you see?"

He shrugged. Her features hardened.

"Jesus god, if you'd just come to me straight after that party—or even on the phone—and told me what you'd done, I would've loved you still. Pissed at you, yes, but ready to understand. We would've worked it out together. Ah, hell, why am I bothering? You don't get it."

"But I do," he said, voice rising in pitch.

"Uh-uhn. Oh, sure, you can say a bunch of words about it, tell me all about some book or movie about it, anything you want but it's not there in your heart. Seems true of a lot of guys, so I guess you're just a plain old regular guy."

"Oh, so because I lied about the party thing and-and all the other stuff, your so-called love got, like, suddenly conditional?"

Her eyes flashed. He didn't know what she was seeing but he didn't like how she was looking at him.

"Don't miss my point," she said through partly clenched teeth. "I would've taken your head off over that party thing, called you every shitty thing under the sun but damn it, I would've at least known you respected me. Maybe we could've come back from that, I don't know. But I wasn't there to be a doormat, some mousy little victim ready to turn herself inside out for you."

"I never asked that," he said, trying to sound defiant and missing by a mile.

"Maybe. But you didn't—you don't really ask for anything."

"What? What are you talking about?" He was struggling to follow her.

"You don't ask or share—you just charge in."

He opened his mouth but nothing came out.

She took a deep breath. "Did you ever think to ask Della to forgive you for following her around, spying on her? Or Dwight for how you treated him like he was some useless dog?"

"Oh, come on, that's—"

"Or ask at the store about the kind of board you were buying or consider asking any of those surfers to teach you? Nope, it was all Roy's way, only Roy's way. The trouble with me is I thought you'd at least come to see me different from all that, ask me to get inside your heart, ask me to let you get really close, but no—not by words and absolutely not by the way you acted."

"Fine, sure, so what about you? What were you asking for?"

She smiled for the first time. "You remember the night you parked out on the road and I was there, waiting for my ride?"

"Of course I do."

"There wasn't any ride. I was waiting for you." She shrugged. "Maybe I was asking you to find me?"

"Okay, so great. I guess I'm supposed to be flattered."

She let the sarcasm go past. "See? You don't even ask why. But I'll tell you anyway: because on the beach you let me bum a smoke and you didn't act like a jerk. You seemed like a genuinely good person and I wanted to get to know you, see who was in there."

"Well, yay for me, huh?"

"Yes, actually: big yay. And I really dug you from the start, Roy. But after that first weekend? I kept getting this feeling I couldn't figure out and finally I realized: weeks later and I was still waiting for you."

"What?" He getting frustrated. "Waiting for me for what?"

"To see me," she said, sharply, then eased back. "Not the Dina you thought I was—or more like decided I was—but the real me. The one you could be completely honest with if you really understood me, if you'd really tried to get there. It's on me, too—I could've tried to tell you but like a girly jerk I was waiting, hoping. I wanted you to get there on your own so I'd know for sure I could trust you. Hell, I even decided if we had sex maybe you'd let go of all this controlling crap, so off with my clothes. Stupid notion that was, huh?"

His elbow began itching again. He didn't bother to scratch.

"This is bullshit!" he shouted right in her face.

"Yeah, I know it is," she said and whirled away.

He grabbed her wrist and held on.

"Let go!" she yelled.

Her cousin was suddenly right there, much bigger than he'd seemed on first take.

"Hey now," the cousin said, holding up a pair of catcher's mitt-sized hands.

Roy quickly released Dina's wrist.

"It's okay, Merle," she said.

The cousin put his hands away but remained close by.

"Roy, I wish you a happy new year, I really do." she said. "But no more letters, no calls, nothing, okay? You just go get yourself a great life."

He couldn't lid the petulance. "Oh well, goll-ly-gee, thanks."

"You're welcome," she said, shaking her head in resignation. "And seriously? I'll be happy for you when you do. If you ever do."

Without a second glance at him, she walked away. Merle trailed along behind with the gait of a patient plow horse.

Dozens of clever retorts surfaced in Roy's mind, then died just as quickly. He wanted to chase after her, shout how much he loved her.

Instead, he walked to the railing and jack-knifed over it, vomiting into the sand.

Roy stayed in that position for what felt like hours. He didn't trust the mayhem in his stomach. He was paralyzed, bloodless.

Finally, he turned and began walking slowly down the boardwalk. The wind was picking up steadily, piercing and chilled. He strained against it, wanting his face to be sanded right down to the skull.

There was a persistent stench riding on the air—dead fish or some road-kill animal, maybe, or both. His guts burbled.

He passed the amusement centers, the pier with the rides, the side street where the pool hall was, the place where a girl had kissed him back so hard one careless night, and Thrasher's with its granite odor of cold oil. Everything was closed, dark, stores boarded up or shuttered.

Ghost City for sure, he thought. I'm the only thing alive. Me and the seagulls.

And Dina, driving away. Dina, gone.

Fine, okay, we're a hundred percent done, have it your way, like it was ever going to be any other way. Fuck it, then. But what in the hell was she talking about? Unconditional love —sounded like that rah-rah-Jesus talk.

Girls! What the hell are they? He was shouting at himself in his head. God damn: they're just on this planet to make us completely crazy. Is she right about all the stuff she said about me? Maybe, but maybe not—I don't know. How do I know? How about I go ask Della: Hey, am I a selfish prick? I am? Oh, okay, so what should I do then? How about I just walk into the ocean and keep going, rid the world of the worst guy ever?

His elbow started itching again. He wanted to scratch it all the way down to bone.

I don't get any of this, he thought, anger subsiding into a low voltage hum. I just can't see the guy they're telling me I am. Who is it they're seeing? Not me, not me, not me tolled the bell in his aching head.

When he reached the end of the boardwalk, he turned and walked back the other way, stopping to gather in the incessant movement and metronome of the ocean, lulled by the rhythm of it, glad at least to have the wind at his back.

His inner ears had begun aching from the cold air. He retreated to his car. It had gotten late; the sun was going.

The car rocked a bit in the gusts, flying sand peppered the windows. Long pulls of the whiskey soon put him to sleep.

A distant explosion yanked him back into the world. Somewhere on the bay side, somebody was shooting off fireworks. Midnight, he realized, swallowing hard against the bile in his throat and wiping the drool off this face.

Firecrackers chattered, cherry bombs pounded and an occasional flash and shriek emanated from a Roman candle zooming up over the rooftops. He got out to watch, his chilled body like a clenched fist slowly uncurling.

Boom, bash, zip: just like that, 1965.

Hey, Dina: got the fireworks, he thought grimly. No violins, though; ho-ho, big joke.

"Happy fucking new year, assholes one and all!" he shouted, shattering the bottle on the street just to add to the noise.

When the fireworks ceased, he drove out of Ocean City at a cortege pace, the heater blasting, windows shut against the stench of dead life and the pale scent of the sea.

He wasn't coming back.

On the highway he tried to reconstruct what Dina had said to him but it was already a blur. The only thing he could do was accept her rejection of him and let himself feel lousy about it.

He knew how to do that, all right, no sweat.

His bedroom beckoned to him, the warmth of his bed, jazz playing through the hours while the ceiling slowly lowered itself over him, casket closing.

He thought of people he knew, looking for some horizon sign: girls he'd dated, then about Dwight, Della, Phil off in basic training or stationed somewhere, friends back from college at their New Year's parties. Prick tease Kimberly. Angela. Jesus, what would she be doing tonight, he wondered, shuddering at images of her being used by a stream of guys or turning up in one of those stag films. Simmons' wife —god, what messed-up world was she living in with that braying jackass?

What were these people to him? Or him to them? He didn't want anything from any of them, didn't want to think about them, or care.

All he could conjure was a rampage to get somewhere where there was no map.

He thought about his parents and their party—it would be long over by the time he got back home, thank god. He could sleep all day if he wanted, maybe watch some bowl games with his father if only they could just sit there and not try to be all goddam meaningful about everything.

He smiled ruefully at himself in the mirror: guess it was Dina who gave me The Talk this time, not you, Dad.

He fiddled with the radio dial, finally bringing in some cornpone station playing saccharine crap. He didn't care—the silence was too awful.

School loomed ahead in another week or so. He knew he should try a bit harder for the spring semester, maybe actually stay on campus a few more days a week, hunker down, stay focused, distract himself somehow. It sparked a weak flame of hope to think that everything and anything was next—all potential and possibility.

He dreamed himself achieving, striving, being one of those people on campus that others admired. Well, okay, that wasn't so likely, but for sure he needed to keep the grades up, get that Associate's degree. After Essex he needed to get into a four-year school, probably Towson—anything to stay out of the draft.

His thoughts kaleidescoped, twenty movies going at the same time. A face took center stage. He shook it away but it tiptoed back.

Some girl in his Chemistry class. Ruthie? No, umm, ah: Rosie. Yeah. Cute. Pony tail. Big pale green eyes, nice body. Very friendly girl, always asking him if he understood the lecture.

"Maybe we could share notes, Roy," she'd said just before Finals. He told her it probably wouldn't help and showed her a portion of a page that was doodled on in Byzantine swirls.

He didn't let her see that the rest of the page was filled with Dina's name.

Rosie had smiled sweetly and bobbed her head at him, pony tail swaying. Cute for sure, but not the girl he wanted.

The next time they talked was just as Finals were ending. "Hey, guess what? I got a C in Chem!" she exclaimed.

"That's really great! I think I got the lowest possible D he could give," he answered with a shrug.

"Aw, it was just one class, Roy," she'd said, patting his shoulder, gazing very intently at him, beaming green-eyed hope. "You'll be okay, I just know it."

"Yeah, right; I couldn't even remember the formula for salt."

"Nackle," she said.

"Huh?"

"I make up words to remember stuff. Nackle is NaCl: Sodium Chloride."

"Oh," he said, smacking his forehead in mock anguish. "Yeah, that's it. Nackle—pretty clever. But even so, why the hell is sodium Na? Who's going to remember that?"

She just grinned into his eyes, her cheeks flushed, clearly finding him very amusing, indeed.

Rosie.

No mistaking that she liked him.

So, he thought, gazing steadily out at the long pour of roadway, maybe ask her out? Get back on the horse kind of thing?

Rosie and Roy. Roy and Rosie. "First comes love, then comes..."

He dismissed it. Ridiculous. Look what you did with the last horse, you dipshit.

He shook his head to clear it.

He was disgusted with himself. Jesus, come on. Put some other girl through his crap? And if he knew anything out of the past six months it was that no girl could save him from screwing up, so what the hell was he thinking? He had to do the changing, figure out what he really wanted and how to find it without hurting another person.

Anyway, school was a few weeks away so best to just keep to himself, he decided, no looking up Rosie's phone number. Though, what was it? Walsh? Right.

He shook his head in frustration. Refocus, he told himself. Stay busy—do you really think you'll get over Dina in a week or a month or a hundred years?

Plan shit, do stuff, occupy your days and nights. Do not go around like some damned sleep-walker.

He hadn't been to the museums in the city recently, so there was that. Or Sherman's—god knew there were so many books yet to read. There were some great films he'd been reading about that were coming to the art houses downtown: Umbrellas of Cherbourg, Woman in the Dunes, Red Desert, The Pawnbroker. He was practically salivating. And, really, did Rosie seem like the art film type? Hell, come to that, maybe he'd meet that very type by going to those films. Somebody wan, willowy and poetic, full of secret lust, with some kind of unidentifiable accent and after the flick—he'd have to remember to say "flick" and not movie—they'd be drinking absinthe in her apartment, Miles playing "'Round About Midnight" on the stereo.

Right. Or maybe he'd just go to the movies and come back home to his bedroom and hide, like usual.

It didn't matter. Just let whatever it is show up. The Turtle Theory, Roy, don't let yourself forget about it: something will come edging over the horizon, you just wait and pretty soon you'll—

A pair of tiny lights sharply gleamed back at him from the highway. He swerved, cursing his voice raw, standing on the brake pedal, seeing the raccoon standing frozen on the road. The car fishtailed toward the shoulder then found a grip on the asphalt. He pulled back into the right lane and eased off the brakes, and came to a stop.

In the rearview he saw the raccoon continue its journey across the road.

He was at the mouth of a side street and turned into it. Parking, he got out and lit a cigarette with shaking hands.

Floods of adrenalin drenched him with sweat. He tried to walk for a moment but his knees buckled.

Roy leaned against the hood of the car, letting the engine heat seep into him, his body's defenses winding down.

He looked up at the night sky, so full of lights in the country darkness—stars, planets. Maybe, he wondered, could there be one where everybody knew what was really going on all the time and not always in a state of total confusion?

Gazing back at the roadway, now grown silvery with his eyes accustomed to the low light, he noticed something colorful in the weeds on the other side of the street.

A child's sock. Pink with little star-shaped flecks of yellow. He picked it up and looked at it in the light of his cigarette.

He thought of Sundays when he was a kid, maybe 12 or 13. The worst day of the week, when his father's sister Caroline and her husband Woody would come over and drill holes through the afternoon with their endlessly trivial talk: work, kids, money, work, money, Sunday after Sunday. In time, Roy was granted permission to go out for a walk or to play. The kids he usually played with were all stuck in their homes, too, so it was him on his own. His first real taste of solitude—keeping company with his own thoughts.

At the end of his street, a long crescent from which the other neighborhood streets emanated like rays, there was a tree that was easy to climb. One Sunday, he found an empty Band-Aid box on his walk and he began collecting roadside discards: a change purse with a broken clasp, some plastic soldiers, a tube of crimson lipstick, odds and ends of coins, a woman's leather glove, soft as a cloud.

He gathered these things week after week and stashed the tin box in the upper limbs of the tree, returning to visit each item in his skyward perch. He had no idea why he collected them except that it tore at him when things were lost, thrown away, left behind. Were they missed? Did some child ache for the lost soldiers, some girl for her lipstick? What happened when things became only their absence?

Roy grimaced, gazing down at the pink and yellow sock. Such a sap, he thought.

He glanced up and down the road for the other sock, hopeful, though how a pair of lost socks could matter more compared to only one was a mystery to him. He only felt the need for retrieval.

The moon was bright and heading for the horizon, causing the trees to cast long arms along the roadway.

He gave up on the second sock.

Home and bed were calling. Maybe Rosie's smile was calling or the next book or film—flick—to devour or something he couldn't imagine. That was the only thing keeping him vaguely balanced: that ever-possible thing, the mystery turtle waiting over the hill.

He ground out his cigarette carefully and started for the car, then turned back to where he'd found the little sock and laid it carefully back on the weedy shoulder. Maybe somebody would come looking for it in the morning, claim it.

He got in the car. Closing the door snipped off the sounds of the outer world. He lingered in the hollow quiet, listening to himself breathe.

Something was ahead, he knew. It was elsewhere but not forever, only waiting, idling.

Okay, he thought, whatever's next. Let's have it.

A chill writhed his body.

He started the car, turning the heater on, leaving the lights off, still savoring the silent gray and black and silver of the dark.

He rolled down his window and watched the whirl overhead, the magic of it filling him up enough to pull in a long draught of cold air and let it replenish him.

He felt wide awake.

About the Author

Courtesy of Peter Hermann

Michael Wright is a playwright, poet, fiction writer, journalist, performance artist and stage director. His poems, plays, and fiction have appeared in such publications as This Land, The Tulsa Voice, The Elvis Monologues, and productions with Heller Theatre (Tulsa), The Vineyard Theatre (NY), Moondance Film Festival, The National Audio Theatre Festival, among others.

His books on writing for performance include Playwriting in Process, Playwriting Master Class and Sensory Writing for Stage and Screen (Hackett Publishers). He is a member of The Dramatists Guild and PEN America.

michaelplaywright.blogspot.com